GLIMMER TRAIN
STORIES

EDITORS
Susan Burmeister-Brown
Linda Davies

CONSULTING EDITORS
Annie Callan
Dave Chipps

COPY EDITOR & PROOFREADER
Scott Allie

TYPESETTING & LAYOUT
Florence McMullen

COVER ILLUSTRATOR
Jane Zwinger

STORY ILLUSTRATOR
Jon Leon

FINAL-PAGE ILLUSTRATOR
Bernard Mulligan, Republic of Ireland

PUBLISHED QUARTERLY
in spring, summer, fall, and winter by
Glimmer Train Press, Inc.
812 SW Washington Street, Suite 1205
Portland, Oregon 97205-3216 U.S.A.
Telephone: 503/221-0836
Facsimile: 503/221-0837

PRINTED IN U.S.A.

Glimmer Train (ISSN #1055-7520), registered in U.S. Patent and Trademark Office, is published quarterly, $29 per year in the U.S., by Glimmer Train Press, Inc., Suite 1205, 812 SW Washington, Portland, OR 97205. Second-class postage paid at Portland, OR, and additional mailing offices. POSTMASTER: Send address changes to Glimmer Train Press, Inc., Suite 1205, 812 SW Washington, Portland, OR 97205.

ISSN # 1055-7520, ISBN # 1-880966-18-2, CPDA BIPAD # 79021

DISTRIBUTION: Bookstores can purchase *Glimmer Train Stories* through these distributors:
    Anderson News Co., 6016 Brookvale Ln., #151, Knoxville, TN 37919
    Baker & Taylor, 652 East Main St., Bridgewater, NJ 08807
    Bernhard DeBoer, Inc., 113 E. Centre St., Nutley, NJ 07110
    Bookpeople, 7900 Edgewater Dr., Oakland, CA 94621
    Ingram Periodicals, 1226 Heil Quaker Blvd., LaVergne, TN 37086
    IPD, 674 Via de la Valle, #204, Solana Beach, CA 92075
    Pacific Pipeline, 8030 S. 228th St., Kent, WA 98032
    Ubiquity, 607 Degraw St., Brooklyn, NY 11217
SUBSCRIPTION SVCS: EBSCO, Faxon, READMORE

Subscription rates: One year, $29 within the U.S. (Visa/MC/check). Airmail to Canada, $39; outside North America, $49. Payable by Visa/MC or check for U.S. dollars drawn on a U.S. bank.

Attention short-story writers: We pay $500 for first publication and onetime anthology rights. Please include a self-addressed, sufficiently-stamped envelope with your submission. **Send manuscripts in January, April, July, and October.** *Send a SASE for guidelines, which will include information on our Short-Story Award for New Writers.*

Dedication

This issue we dedicate to our father,
born Helmut Johann Theodor Burmeister,
renamed Henry John Burmeister in 1927 when he
immigrated to this country at the age of ten.
He will turn seventy-nine this summer.

We asked him last night to name the books that have
most stayed with him, and his answer was quick:
Les Miserables, by Victor Hugo,
My Country and My People, by Lin Yutang,
the Old Testament,
and, as a young man, the Horatio Alger books.

Sometimes in the faces of our loved ones, we can see
their favorite books.

Happy Birthday to you, Pop.
We love you.

Susan & Linde

CONTENTS

Junot Díaz
Invierno
7

Nomi Eve
Esther and Yochanan
27

Article by Siobhan Dowd
Writer Detained: Wei Jingsheng
40

Lara Stapleton
The Lowest Blue Flame Before Nothing
45

Essay by Annie Callan
Writing out of Ireland:
A Terrible Beauty Is Reborn
61

Mary Brockman
What Is She Like?
83

Abigail Thomas
Herb's Pajamas
85

$\mathscr{C}$ONTENTS

Interview with Thom Jones
Short-story writer and novelist-in-training
91

Noy Holland
Someone Is Always Missing
109

Interview with Barbara Scot
Untangling the threads
123

Gary D. Wilson
A Middle-Aged Man
135

The Last Pages
152

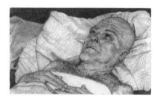

Past Authors and Artists
159

What a collection!
160

Junot Díaz

*Me, before I came to the States. Already sensed
that something was about to go wrong, though.*

Junot Díaz lives in Brooklyn and his fiction has appeared in *Story*, *The New Yorker* and *Time-Out*. His collection of stories will be published by Riverhead Books in the summer of this year.

JUNOT DÍAZ
Invierno

From the top of Westminister, our main strip, you could see the thinnest sliver of ocean cresting the horizon to the east. My father had been shown that sight—the management showed everyone—but as he drove us in from JFK he didn't stop to point it out. The ocean might have made us feel better, considering what else there was to see. London Terrace itself was a mess; half the buildings still needed their wiring and in the evening light these structures sprawled about the landscape like ships of brick that had run aground. Mud followed gravel everywhere and the grass, planted late in fall, poked out of the snow in dead tufts.

Each building has its own laundry room, Papi said. Mami looked vaguely out of the snout of her parka and nodded. That's wonderful, she said. I was watching the snow sift over itself and my brother was cracking his knuckles. This was our first day in the States. The world was frozen solid.

Our apartment seemed huge to us. Rafa and I had a room to ourselves and the kitchen, with its refrigerator and stove, was about the size of our house on Sumner Welles. We didn't stop shivering until Papi set the apartment temperature to about eighty. Beads of water gathered on the windows like bees and we had to wipe the glass to see outside. Rafa and I were stylish in our new clothes and we wanted out, but Papi told us to take off our boots and our parkas. He sat us down in front of the television, his arms lean and surprisingly hairy right up to the short-cut sleeves. He had just shown us how to flush the toilets, run the sinks, and start the shower.

This isn't a slum, Papi began. I want you to treat everything around you with respect. I don't want you throwing any of your garbage on the floor or on the street. I don't want you going to the bathroom in the bushes.

Rafa nudged me. In Santo Domingo I'd pissed everywhere, and the first time Papi had seen me in action, whizzing on a street corner, on the night of his triumphant return, he had said, What are you doing?

Decent people live around here and that's how we're going to live. You're Americans now. He had his Chivas Regal bottle on his knee.

After waiting a few seconds to show that yes, I'd digested everything he'd said, I asked, Can we go out now?

Why don't you help me unpack? Mami suggested. Her hands were very still; usually they were fussing with a piece of paper, a sleeve, or each other.

We'll just be out for a little while, I said. I got up and pulled on my boots. Had I known my father even a little I might not have turned my back on him. But I didn't know him; he'd spent the last five years in the States working, and we'd spent the last five years in Santo Domingo waiting. He grabbed my ear and wrenched me back onto the couch. He did not look happy.

You'll go out when I tell you you're ready. I don't want either of you getting lost or getting hurt out there. You don't know this place.

I looked over at Rafa, who sat quietly in front of the TV. Back on the island, the two of us had taken guaguas clear across the Capital by ourselves. I looked up at Papi, his narrow face still unfamiliar. Don't you eye me, he said.

Mami stood up. You kids might as well give me a hand.

I didn't move. On the TV the newscasters were making small, flat noises at each other.

Since we weren't allowed out of the house—it's too cold, Papi said—we mostly sat in front of the TV or stared out at the snow those first days. Mami cleaned everything about ten times and made us some damn elaborate lunches.

Pretty early on Mami decided that watching TV was beneficial; you could learn English from it. She saw our young minds as bright, spiky sunflowers in need of light, and arranged us as close to the TV as possible to maximize our exposure. We watched the news, sitcoms, cartoons, *Tarzan, Flash Gordon, Jonny Quest, Herculoids, Sesame Street*—eight, nine hours of TV a day, but it was *Sesame Street* that gave us our best lessons. Each word my brother and I learned we passed between ourselves, repeating over and over, and when Mami asked us to show her how to say it, we shook our heads and said, Don't worry about it.

Just tell me, she said, and when we pronounced the words slowly, forming huge, lazy soap-bubbles of sound, she never could duplicate them. Her lips seemed to tug apart even the simplest constructions. That sounds horrible, I said.

What do you know about English? she asked.

At dinner she'd try her English out on Papi, but he just poked at his pernil, which was not my mother's best dish.

I can't understand a word you're saying, he said one night. Mami had cooked rice with squid. It's best if I take care of the English.

How do you expect me to learn?

You don't have to learn, he said. Besides, the average woman can't learn English.

Oh?

It's a difficult language to master, he said, first in Spanish and then in English.

Mami didn't say another word. In the morning, as soon as Papi was out of the apartment, Mami turned on the TV and put us in front of it. The apartment was always cold in the morning and leaving our beds was a serious torment.

It's too early, we said.

It's like school, she suggested.

No, it's not, we said. We were used to going to school at noon.

You two complain too much. She would stand behind us and when I turned around she would be mouthing the words we were learning, trying to make sense of them.

Even Papi's early-morning noises were strange to me. I lay in bed, listening to him stumbling around in the bathroom, like he was drunk or something. I didn't know what he did for Reynolds Aluminum, but he had a lot of uniforms in his closet, all filthy with machine oil.

I had expected a different father, one about seven feet tall with enough money to buy our entire barrio, but this one was average height, with an average face. He'd come to our house in Santo Domingo in a busted-up taxi and the gifts he had brought us were small things—toy guns and tops—that we were too old for, that we broke right away. Even though he hugged us and took us out to dinner on the Malecón—our first meat in years—I didn't know what to make of him. A father is a hard thing to get to know.

Those first weeks in the States, Papi spent a great deal of his home-time downstairs with his books or in front of the TV. He said little to us that wasn't disciplinary, which didn't surprise us. We'd seen other dads in action, understood that part of the drill.

What he got on me about the most was my shoelaces. Papi had a thing with shoelaces. I didn't know how to tie them properly, and when I put together a rather formidable knot, Papi would bend down and pull it apart with one tug. At least you have a future as a magician, Rafa said, but this was serious. Rafa showed me how, and I said, Fine, and had no problems in front of him, but when Papi was breathing down my neck, his hand on a belt, I couldn't perform; I looked at my father like my laces were live wires he wanted me to touch together.

I met some dumb men in the Guardia, Papi said, but every single one of them could tie his motherfucking shoes. He looked over at Mami. Why can't he?

These were not the sort of questions that had answers. She looked down, studied the veins that threaded the backs of her hands. For a second Papi's watery turtle-eyes met mine. Don't you look at me, he said.

Even on days I managed a halfway decent retard knot, as Rafa called them, Papi still had my hair to go on about. While Rafa's hair was straight and dark and glided through a comb like a Caribbean grandparent's dream, my hair still had enough of the African to condemn me to endless combings and out-of-this-world haircuts. My mother cut our hair every month, but this time when she put me in the chair my father told her not to bother.

Only one thing will take care of that, he said. Yunior, go get dressed.

Rafa followed me into my bedroom and watched while I buttoned my shirt. His mouth was tight. I started to feel anxious. What's your problem? I said.

Nothing.

Then stop watching me. When I got to my shoes, he tied them for me. At the door my father looked down and said, You're getting better.

I knew where the van was parked but I went the other way just to catch a glimpse of the neighborhood. Papi didn't notice my defection until I had rounded the corner, and when he growled my name I hurried back, but I had already seen the fields and the children on the snow.

I sat in the front seat. He popped a tape of Jonny Ventura into the player and took us out smoothly to Route 9. The snow lay in dirty piles on the side of the road. There can't be anything worse than old snow, he said. It's nice while it falls but once it gets to the ground it just causes trouble.

Are there accidents?

Not with me driving.

The cattails on the banks of the Raritan were stiff and the color of sand, and when we crossed the river, Papi said, I work in the next town.

We were in Perth Amboy for the services of a real talent, a Puerto Rican barber named Rubio who knew just what to do with the pelo malo. He put two or three creams on my head and had me sit with the foam awhile; after his wife rinsed me off he studied my head in the mirror, tugged at my hair, rubbed an oil into it, and finally sighed.

It's better to shave it all off, Papi said.

I have some other things that might work.

Papi looked at his watch. Shave it.

All right, Rubio said. I watched the clippers plow through my hair, watched my scalp appear, tender and defenseless. One of the old men in the waiting area snorted and held his paper higher. When he was finished Rubio massaged talcum powder on my neck. Now you look guapo, he said. He handed me a stick of gum, which would go right to my brother.

Well? Papi asked. I nodded. As soon as we were outside the cold clamped down on my head like a slab of wet dirt.

We drove back in silence. An oil tanker was pulling into port on the Raritan and I wondered how easy it would be for me to slip aboard and disappear.

Do you like negras? my father asked.

I turned my head to look at the women we had just passed. I turned back and realized that he was waiting for an answer, that he wanted to know, and while I wanted to blurt that I didn't like girls in any denomination, I said instead, Oh yes, and he smiled.

They're beautiful, he said, and lit a cigarette. They'll take care of you better than anyone.

Rafa laughed when he saw me. You look like a big thumb.

Dios mío, Mami said, turning me around.

It looks good, Papi said.

And the cold's going to make him sick.

Papi put his cold palm on my head. He likes it fine, he said.

Papi worked a long fifty-hour week and on his days off he expected quiet, but my brother and I had too much energy to be quiet; we didn't think anything of using our sofas for trampolines at nine in the morning, while Papi was asleep. In our old barrio we were accustomed to folks shocking the streets with merengue twenty-four hours a day. Our upstairs neighbors, who themselves fought like trolls over everything, would stomp down on us. Will you two please shut up? and then Papi would come out of his room, his shorts unbuttoned and say, What did I tell you? How many times have I told you to keep it quiet? He was free with his smacks and we spent whole afternoons on Punishment Row—our bedroom—where we had to lie on our beds and not get off, because if he burst in and caught us at the window, staring out at the beautiful snow, he would pull our ears and smack us, and then we would have to kneel in the corner for a few hours. If we messed that up, joking around or cheating, he would force us to kneel down on the cutting side of a coconut grater, and only when we were bleeding and whimpering would he let us up.

Now you'll be quiet, he'd say, satisfied, and we'd lay in bed, our knees burning with iodine, and wait for him to go to work so we could put our hands against the cold glass.

We watched the neighborhood children building snowmen and igloos, having snowball fights. I told my brother about the field I'd seen, vast in my memory, but he just shrugged. A brother and sister lived across in apartment four, and when they were out we would wave to them. They waved to us and motioned for us to come out but we shook our heads, We can't.

The brother shrugged, and tugged his sister out to where the other children were, with their shovels and their long, snow-encrusted scarves. She seemed to like Rafa, and waved to him as she walked off. He didn't wave back.

North American girls are supposed to be beautiful, he said. Have you seen any?

What do you call her? He reached down for a tissue and sneezed out a double-barrel of snot. All of us had headaches and colds and coughs; even with the heat cranked up, winter was kicking our asses. I had to wear a Christmas hat around the apartment to keep my shaven head warm; I looked like an unhappy tropical elf.

I wiped my nose. If this is the United States, mail me home.

Don't worry, Mami says. We're probably going home.

How does she know?

Her and Papi have been talking about it. She thinks it would be better if we went back. Rafa ran a finger glumly over our window; he didn't want to go; he liked the TV and the toilet and already saw himself with the girl in apartment four.

I don't know about that, I said. Papi doesn't look like he's going anywhere.

What do you know? You're just a little mojón.

I know more than you, I said. Papi had never once mentioned going back to the Island. I waited to get him in a good mood, after he had watched *Abbott and Costello,* and asked him if he thought we would be going back soon.

For what?

A visit.

Maybe, he grunted. Maybe not. Don't plan on it.

By the third week I was worried we weren't going to make it.

Mami, who had been our authority on the Island, was dwin-dling. She cooked our food and then sat there, waiting to wash the dishes. She had no friends, no neighbors to visit. You should talk to me, she said, but we told her to wait for Papi to get home. He'll talk to you, I guaranteed. Rafa's temper, which was sometimes a problem, got worse. I would tug at his hair, an old game of ours, and he would explode. We fought and fought and fought and after my mother pried us apart, instead of making up like the old days, we sat scowling on opposite sides of our room and planned each other's demise. I'm going to burn you alive, he promised. You should number your limbs, cabrón, I told

him, so they'll know how to put you back together for the funeral. We squirted acid at each other with our eyes, like reptiles. Our boredom made everything worse.

One day I saw the brother and sister from apartment four

gearing up to go play, and instead of waving I pulled on my parka. Rafa was sitting on the couch, flipping between a Chinese cooking show and an all-star Little League game. I'm going out, I told him.

Sure you are, he said, but when I pushed open the front door, he said, Hey!

The air outside was very cold and I nearly fell down our steps. No one in the neighborhood was the shoveling type. Throwing my scarf over my mouth, I stumbled across the uneven crust of snow. I caught up to the brother and sister on the side of our building.

Wait up! I yelled. I want to play with you.

The brother watched me with a half grin, not understanding a word I'd said, his arms scrunched nervously at his side. His hair was a frightening no-color. His sister had the greenest eyes and her freckled face was cowled in a hood of pink fur. We had on the same brand of mittens, bought cheap from Two Guys. I stopped and we faced each other, our white breath nearly reaching across the distance between us. The world was ice and the ice burned with sunlight. This was my first real encounter with North Americans and I felt loose and capable on that plain of ice. I motioned with my mittens and smiled. The sister turned to her brother and laughed. He said something to her and then she ran to where the other children were, the peals of her laughter trailing over her shoulder like the spumes of her hot breath.

I've been meaning to come out, I said. But my father won't let us right now. He thinks we're too young, but look, I'm older than your sister, and my brother looks older than you.

The brother pointed at himself. Eric, he said.

My name's Joaquín, I said.

Juan, he said.

No, Joaquín, I repeated. Don't they teach you guys how to speak?

His grin never faded. Turning, he walked over to the approaching group of children. I knew that Rafa was watching me from the window and fought the urge to turn around and wave. The gringo children watched me from a distance and then walked away. Wait, I said, but then an Oldsmobile pulled into the next lot, its tires muddy and thick with snow. I couldn't follow them. The sister looked back once, a lick of her hair peeking out of her hood. After they had gone, I stood in the snow until my feet were cold. I was too afraid of getting my ass beat to go any farther.

Was it fun? Rafa was sprawled in front of the TV.

Hijo de la gran puta, I said, sitting down.

You look frozen.

I didn't answer him. We watched TV until a snowball struck the glass patio door and both of us jumped.

What was that? Mami wanted to know from her room.

Two more snowballs exploded on the glass. I peeked behind the curtain and saw the brother and the sister hiding behind a snow-buried Dodge.

Nothing, Señora, Rafa said. It's just the snow.

What, is it learning how to dance out there?

It's just falling, Rafa said.

We both stood behind the curtain, and watched the brother throw fast and hard, like a pitcher.

Each day the trucks would roll into our neighborhood with the garbage. The landfill stood two miles out, but the mechanics of the winter air conducted its sound and smells to us undiluted. When we opened a window we could hear the bulldozers spreading the garbage out in thick, putrid layers across the top of the landfill. We could see the gulls attending the mound, thousands of them, wheeling.

Do you think kids play out there? I asked Rafa. We were standing on the porch, brave; at any moment Papi could pull into the parking lot and see us.

Of course they do. Wouldn't you?

I licked my lips. They must find a lot of crap out there.

Plenty, Rafa said.

That night I dreamed of home, that we'd never left. I woke up, my throat aching, hot with fever. I washed my face in the sink, then sat next to our window, my brother snoring, and watched the pebbles of ice falling and freezing into a shell over the cars and the snow and the pavement. Learning to sleep in new places was an ability you were supposed to lose as you grew older, but I never had it. The building was only now settling into itself; the tight magic of the just-hammered-in nail was finally relaxing. I heard someone walking around in the living room and when I went out I found my mother standing in front of the patio door.

You can't sleep? she asked, her face smooth and perfect in the glare of the halogens.

I shook my head.

We've always been alike that way, she said. That won't make your life any easier.

I put my arms around her waist. That morning alone we'd seen three moving trucks from our patio door. I'm going to pray for Dominicans, she had said, her face against the glass, but what we would end up getting were Puerto Ricans.

She must have put me to bed because the next day I woke up next to Rafa. He was snoring. Papi was in the next room snoring as well, and something inside of me told me that I wasn't a quiet sleeper.

At the end of the month the bulldozers capped the landfill with a head of soft, blond dirt, and the evicted gulls flocked over the development, shitting and fussing, until the first of the new garbage was brought in.

My brother was bucking to be Number One Son; in all other

things he was generally unchanged, but when it came to my father he listened with a scrupulousness he had never afforded our mother. Papi said he wanted us inside, Rafa stayed inside. I was less attentive; I played in the snow for short stretches, though never out of sight of the apartment. You're going to get caught, Rafa forecasted. I could tell that my boldness made him miserable; from our windows he watched me packing snow and throwing myself into drifts. I stayed away from the gringos. When I saw the brother and sister from apartment four, I stopped farting around and watched for a sneak attack. Eric waved and his sister waved; I didn't wave back. Once he came over and showed me the baseball he must have just gotten. Roberto Clemente, he said, but I went on with building my fort. His sister grew flushed and said something loud and rude and then Eric sighed. Neither of them were handsome children.

One day the sister was out by herself and I followed her to the field. Huge concrete pipes sprawled here and there on the snow. She ducked into one of these and I followed her, crawling on my knees.

She sat in the pipe, crosslegged and grinning. She took her hands out of her mittens and rubbed them together. We were out of the wind and I followed her example. She poked a finger at me.

Joaquín, I said. All my friends call me Yunior.

Joaquín Yunior, she said. Elaine. Elaine Pitt.

Elaine.

Joaquín.

It's really cold, I said, my teeth chattering.

She said something and then felt the ends of my fingers. Cold, she said.

I knew that word already. I nodded. Frío. She showed me how to put my fingers in my armpits.

Warm, she said.

Yes, I said. Very warm.

At night, Mami and Papi talked. He sat on his side of the table and she leaned close, asking him, Do you ever plan on taking these children out? You can't keep them sealed up like this; they aren't dead yet.

They'll be going to school soon, he said, sucking on his pipe. And as soon as winter lets up I want to show you the ocean. You can see it around here, you know, but it's better to see it up close.

How much longer does winter last?

Not long, he promised. You'll see. In a few months none of you will remember this and by then I won't have to work too much. We'll be able to travel in spring and see everything.

I hope so, Mami said.

My mother was not a woman easily cowed, but in the States she let my father roll over her. If he said he had to be at work for two days straight, she said okay and cooked enough moro to last him. She was depressed and sad and missed her father and her friends. Everyone had warned her that the U.S. was a difficult place where even the devil got his ass beat, but no one had told her that she would have to spend the rest of her natural life snowbound with her children. She wrote letter after letter home, begging her sisters to come as soon as possible. I need the company, she explained. This neighborhood is empty and friendless. And she begged Papi to bring his friends over. She wanted to talk about unimportant matters, and see a brown face who didn't call her mother or wife.

None of you are ready for guests, Papi said. Look at this house. Look at your children. Me dan vergüenza to see them slouching around like that.

You can't complain about this apartment. All I do is clean it.

What about your sons?

My mother looked over at me and then at Rafa. I put one shoe over the other. After that, she had Rafa keep after me about my shoelaces. When we heard the van arriving in the parking lot, Mami called us over for a quick inspection. Hair, teeth, hands, feet. If anything was wrong she'd hide us in the bathroom until it was fixed. Her dinners grew elaborate. She even changed the TV for Papi without calling him a zángano.

Okay, he said finally. Maybe it can work.

It doesn't have to be that big a production, Mami said.

Two Fridays in a row he brought a friend over for dinner and Mami put on her best polyester jumpsuit and got us spiffy in our red pants, thick white belts, and amaranth-blue Chams shirts. Seeing her asthmatic with excitement made us hopeful that our world was about to be transformed, but these were awkward dinners. The men were bachelors and divided their time between talking to Papi and eyeing Mami's ass. Papi seemed to enjoy their company but Mami spent her time on her feet, hustling food to the table, opening beers, and changing the channel. She started out each night natural and unreserved, with a face that scowled as easily as it grinned, but as the men loosened their belts and aired out their toes and talked their talk, she withdrew; her expressions narrowed until all that remained was a tight, guarded smile that seemed to drift across the room the way a splash of sunlight glides across a wall. We kids were ignored for the most part, except once, when the first man, Miguel, asked, Can you two box as well as your father?

They're fine fighters, Papi said.

Your father is very fast. Has good hand speed. Miguel shook his head, laughing. I saw him finish this one tipo. He put fulano on his ass.

That *was* funny, Papi agreed. Miguel had brought a bottle of Bermúdez rum; he and Papi were drunk.

It's time you go to your room, Mami said, touching my shoulder.

Why? I asked. All we do is sit there.

That's how I feel about my home, Miguel said.

Mami's glare cut me in half. Such a fresh mouth, she said, shoving us toward our room. We sat, as predicted, and listened.

On both visits, the men ate their fill, congratulated Mami on her cooking, Papi on his sons, and then stayed about an hour for propriety's sake. Cigarettes, dominos, gossip, and then the inevitable, Well, I have to get going. We have work tomorrow. You know how that is.

Of course I do. What else do we Dominicans know?

Afterward, Mami cleaned the pans quietly in the kitchen, scraping at the roasted pig flesh, while Papi sat out on our front porch in his short sleeves; he seemed to have grown impervious to the cold these last five years. When he came inside, he showered and pulled on his overalls. I have to work tonight, he said.

Mami stopped scratching at the pans with a spoon. You should find yourself a more regular job.

Papi smiled. Maybe I will.

As soon as he left, Mami ripped the needle from the album and interrupted Felix de Rosario. We heard her in the closet, pulling on her coat and her boots.

Do you think she's leaving us? I asked.

Rafa wrinkled his brow. It's a possibility, he said. What would you do if you were her?

I'd already be in Santo Domingo.

When we heard the front door open, we let ourselves out of our room and found the apartment empty.

We better go after her, I said.

Rafa stopped at the door. Let's give her a minute, he said.

What's wrong with you? She's probably face down in the snow.

We'll wait two minutes, he said.

Shall I count?

Don't be a wiseguy.

One, I said loudly. He pressed his face against the glass patio door. We were about to hit the door when she returned, panting, an envelope of cold around her.

Where did you get to? I asked.

I went for a walk. She dropped her coat at the door; her face was red from the cold and she was breathing deeply, as if she'd sprinted the last thirty steps.

Where?

Just around the corner.

Why the hell did you do that?

She started to cry, and when Rafa put his hand on her waist, she slapped it away. We went back to our room.

I think she's losing it, I said.

She's just lonely, Rafa said.

The night before the snowstorm I heard the wind at our window. I woke up the next morning, freezing. Mami was fiddling with the thermostat; we could hear the gurgle of water in the pipes but the apartment didn't get much warmer.

Just go play, Mami said. That will keep your mind off it.

Is it broken?

I don't know. She looked at the knob dubiously. Maybe it's slow this morning.

None of the gringos were outside playing. We sat by the window and waited for them. In the afternoon my father called from work; I could hear the forklifts when I answered.

Rafa?

No, it's me.

Get your mother.

How are you doing?

Get your mother.

We got a big storm on the way, he explained to her—even from where I was standing I could hear his voice. There's no way I can get out to see you. It's gonna be bad. Maybe I'll get there tomorrow.

What should I do?

Just keep indoors. And fill the tub with water.

Where are you sleeping? Mami asked.

At a friend's.

She turned her face from us. Okay, she said. When she got off the phone she sat in front of the TV. She could see I was going to pester her about Papi; she told me, Just watch the TV.

Radio WADO recommended spare blankets, water, flashlights, and food. We had none of these things. What happens if we get buried? I asked. Will we die? Will they have to save us in boats?

I don't know, Rafa said. I don't know anything about snow. I was spooking him. He went over to the window and peeked out.

We'll be fine, Mami said. As long as we're warm. She went over and raised the heat again.

But what if we get buried?

You can't have that much snow.

How do you know?

Because twelve inches isn't going to bury anybody, even a pain-in-the-ass like you.

I went out on the porch and watched the first snow begin to fall like finely-sifted ash. If we die, Papi's going to feel bad, I said.

Don't talk about it like that, Rafa said.

Mami turned away and laughed.

Four inches fell in an hour and the snow kept falling.

Mami waited until we were in bed, but I heard the door and woke Rafa. She's at it again, I said.

Outside?

You know it.

He put on his boots grimly. He paused at the door and then looked back at the empty apartment. Let's go, he said.

She was standing on the edge of the parking lot, ready to cross Westminister. The apartment lamps glared on the frozen ground and our breath was white in the night air. The snow was gusting.

Go home, she said.

We didn't move.

Did you at least lock the front door? she asked.

Rafa shook his head.

It's too cold for thieves anyway, I said.

Mami smiled and nearly slipped on the sidewalk. I'm not good at walking on this vaina.

I'm real good, I said. Just hold onto me.

We crossed Westminister. The cars were moving very slowly and the wind was loud and full of snow.

This isn't too bad, I said. These people should see a hurricane.

Where should we go? Rafa asked. He was blinking a lot to keep the snow out of his eyes.

Go straight, Mami said. That way we don't get lost.

We should mark the ice.

She put her hands around us both. It's easier if we go straight.

We went down to the edge of the apartments and looked out over the landfill, a misshapen, shadowy mound that abutted the Raritan. Rubbish fires burned all over it like sores and the dump trucks and bulldozers slept quietly and reverently at its base. It smelled like something the river had tossed out from its floor, something moist and heaving. We found the basketball courts next and the pool, empty of water, and Parkridge, the next neighborhood over, which was full and had many, many children. We even saw the ocean, up there at the top of Westminister, like the blade of a long, curved knife. Mami was crying but we pretended not to notice. We threw snowballs at the sliding cars and once I removed my cap just to feel the snowflakes scatter across my cold, hard scalp.

Nomi Eve

*Me, in Jerusalem, eating ice cream, 1977. That's my aunt Ada
snoozing in the background.*

Nomi Eve is a twenty-seven-year-old fiction writer currently living in Israel.
Two of her stories have been published in the *Village Voice Literary Supplement*.
She has an MFA in fiction writing from Brown University, and has worked
as a freelance book reviewer for the *Village Voice*, the *Boston Globe*, *New York
Newsday*, the *Jerusalem Post*, and *Publishers' Weekly*.

Eve is writing her first novel, entitled *The Double Tree*, in which "Esther and
Yochanan" appears in a self-contained section.

NOMI EVE
Esther and Yochanan

My father has researched our family history all the way back to the seventeenth century. What I am doing is juxtaposing his written family history with my own fiction. Everything my father has written is true. Everything I write is what I imagine.

My father writes:

Rabbi Yochanan Schine, a student of the famous Chatam Sofer, was engaged to Esther Sophie Goldiner Hersch, the granddaughter of the Chief Rabbi of the British Empire. Esther and Yochanan were my great great grandparents. They migrated to Israel and married in 1838 in Jerusalem.

I write:

Esther was pious but in a peripheral way. She knew the mitzvot, she knew to make the Sabbath holy, but she felt that there was no real harm in putting her own creative interpretation on the old rules because certainly creativity was an essential and blessed quality of Man and it would be a sin not to use it.

At first she did not like Jerusalem; she was from a long line of people who lacked sense of direction. The stony city, with all of its obscurant walls, twists, and turns seemed to her a nasty place without any recognizable plan.

Four months and two days after the young couple arrived, she ventured out alone for the first time. Quickly lost, but not frightened, Esther decided she would just wander. She knew that if she wanted to, she could ask someone to show her the way back to their house, which was a half-grand, half-decrepit habitation on Rev Pinchas Street. It was located across from the American colony house in the center of town.

And then Esther smelled the bread. She walked forward, turned a corner, continued forward a few more steps. Soon she was standing outside an arched open door watching a baker slide a tray of dough into a furnace. Esther stood and stared. The steam and sweat and dough and bare baker skin created in the room an atmosphere magnetic, carnally alluring. The baker was a young man, no more than twenty. Esther, married less than four months, was nineteen.

Although she was not ordinarily a believer in astrology, and had absolutely no idea how sailors used the night sky to tell them where to go, she felt certain that crucial stars had descended into that tiny bakery room, and though not of the glowing sort, had managed to not only mystic the moment but also to make for her a perfect navigational tool. In short, she was inspired, and knew for once in her life, exactly in which direction she was supposed to go.

The baker stood before her—a destination slim and brown. He was lithe and beautiful in a coltish, boyish way. Small. Only a bit taller than she. Esther immediately took in his huge almondy eyes, and his hair—thick dark brown hair gathered in a low braid at the back. He seemed to her like something carved out of precious wood; miniature, masculine, and muscular and all at once.

The bakery was only two rooms: one with a low wooden baking table rutted and eternally floury from years of use, and the other with a brick furnace that had been hewn, by the baker's grandfather, out of the limestone wall. It was behind what would later be the Russian Compound but was then a rubbly clump of lower-class homes bordering the more prosperous center of town. When the baker saw the young woman with the full skirt, cinched at the waist, when he saw the big brown eyes of the woman, when he saw her white skin, full lips, and attractive face, he invited her in. He gave her a fresh roll and asked her, in nervous, clumsy Yiddish (which like a mule kicked and brayed itself off of his tongue; he was embarrassed at his language's lack of manners) if she would like some sweet mint tea. This was the start of her nine-year love affair with the baker and life-long passionate entanglement with Jerusalem, the city whose twists, turns, bakers, and twin arcane whispers of piety and perversity ultimately spoke straight to her heart.

Esther would make love with her husband at night "through her front door," and then, in the daytime, she carried out an affair with the baker, a third-generation Palestinian Jew who had a voice that made her think, for no good reason, of clouds. Their sexual game was ruled by the fact that the baker would only enter into her "rear door." Both euphemism (which in the entire nine years they never breached) and position (which in the entire nine years they never varied except slightly in angle) suited each of them, titillating not only the tenderest parts of their anatomies, but also the deeply humorous sense of sex that they found they shared.

She came once a week, on Tuesdays, in the late afternoon when her husband would be busy participating in his civic meetings, and the rest of the town, in classic Mediterranean style, would be indoors either scheming, studying, or sleeping. The baker, whose hands Esther always thought were strangely thin-fingered, uncallused, for a baker, would lock the door to the back of the shop. And as he walked over to her, she would be laying a clean cloth down on the baking table. She loved lifting a finger to his lips, putting her fingers in his mouth, and then with her wet fingers she would trace the graceful outline of his face, from mouth to nose, eyes, and into ears.

Always, when they were both ready, she would turn away from him and lean her body over the table. He pulled up her skirts, down her undergarments, and down his own pants. Then he licked the fingers on his right hand and slowly, passionately opened her up. Soon he slid right into her. She loved the feel of his body angling its way upward. She loved the feel of her fullheavy breasts hard pressing into the wooden table. He gripped her buttocks and thrust himself deep.

They kissed and panted and hungered at and for each other's skin, more, not less fervently as the years went by. Theirs, they agreed, was an ancient elemental passion that must have existed, like sand, earth, and sky, long before either of them had been born. And despite the intense physicality of their togethering, both Esther and the baker always felt insubstantial, flimsy, oh so light in the presence of this passion. But this was not a bad feeling. When they made love it was as if they were wrapping their bodies not only around each other but also, and more essentially, around something else that had before been naked. It was, they agreed, as if the passion were the real creature and they, though temporarily deprived of the normal trappings of personhood, were lucky to have been chosen as its favorite clothes. They dressed the passion in carnal finery, and the passion wore them with secret frequency.

My great great great grandmother, Esther Sophie Goldner Schine, granddaughter of the Chief Rabbi of the British Empire, thought her husband's coming in through her front door and her lover's coming in through her rear door was the perfect arrangement for a Jewish woman. Something about the notion of separate facilities fit nicely into the ready framework of Kashrut. Milk here, meat there, and as long as there was proper distance between things, everything stayed quietly kosher.

My father writes:

Yochanan came from a part of East Prussia called Sheinlanka, which means "pretty terraces." Today it is part of Poland, not far from the town of Posnan. He came to Israel under the following circumstances:

In 1836, the Chief Rabbi of the British Empire wrote to a famous

30   *Glimmer Train Stories*

Prussian Rabbi by the name of the Chatam Sofer, and asked for a shidach for his granddaughter Esther, under the condition that the young couple move to Israel. A shidach is the Yiddish term for a marriage match. This was before the existence of Zionism. Most Jews still believed that Israel should not and could not be established until the Messiah came.

The Chief Rabbi disagreed with prevailing thought. He was among a group of radical, European, liberal Orthodox Jews who believed that moving to Israel was not in opposition to the messianic idea. The Chief Rabbi wrote to the Chatam Sofer because he knew that this Rabbi was also of this thinking.

The Chatam Sofer sent his favorite student, Yochanan, whose father was himself a great scholar.

I write:

On the second Tuesday in Iyar, four months after they arrived in Jerusalem, Yochanan finished early with his civic meeting and decided to make for home. He was just about to walk past the American Colony when he saw Esther step out of the front door of their house and turn to walk the other way. It was late fall, and chilly. She was wearing her long maroon coat and the wide-brimmed black hat that tipped down over her right eye and made her vision, she always explained, "a bit drunk feeling, you know, only half there and wobbly, but not too bad, I find my way after all." Yochanan loved his wife's way of speaking. Her sentences were curvy and full of original character.

Yochanan called out to Esther but he was too far for her to hear and so he walked on and meant to call again, but then he found himself walking quietly, stealthily, after his wife around a corner, and again, another corner, and then down the street and into an alley. He stopped at the mouth of the alley and watched his wife walk through the bakery back door. Her maroon coat wafted behind her for several seconds and then too, disappeared into the warm realm of dough and yeast.

Pulling back and into a doorway on which was graffitied the word *Sky* in sloppy Aramaic, he looked up at the real sky, which was darkening with the foredream of a storm. He watched as the baker poked his head out and then shut the front door of his shop. Hidden, but only ten feet away, Yochanan didn't say a word. Then he walked to the closed bakery door and put his ear to the old wood of it. Soon he could hear his wife groaning. He stepped away from the door and looked up and down the street. No one was in the alley, nor walking towards it. He walked back and listened some more. He became aroused almost immediately, and soon was picturing the baker holding Esther's naked breasts, petting them gently and then lifting up the nipples to his mouth. First one and then the other. And the baker's hand, Yochanan imagined the baker's left hand reaching in between Esther's legs, which she pressed together tightly. Soon, in his mind, they were pressing their naked bodies together and moving, back and forth, toward and away, with the tempestuous ease of a storm just brewing. The storm outside began to blow. Yochanan huddled into his coat, raised his collar, and ducked deeper into the doorway. Shutting his eyes, he leaned into the images as if they were the real door, open and welcoming, while the wooden one, closed and cold against his body, kept him out of all this. Now he heard the baker groaning. Esther let out a small passionate yelp. And as the two lovers inside reached satiety, the one outside reached down and touched himself, pressed there, pressed and pulled himself to solitary, intense pleasure. Only then did he leave.

Yochanan put his hands over his hat and ran through the rain. His feet swish-swished into puddles already forming in the narrow, stony streets. As he ran, an angry litany, like an opposite prayer, wrote itself on his brain:

32   *Glimmer Train Stories*

The baker has a face of mouldy clay.
The baker has hands of heavy, stinking wood.
The baker is a deformed gentile in disguise.
The baker is an eater of clams.
A descendant of Amalake.
The devil of devils.
The baker is ... the baker is ... the baker is shtupping my wife!

The rain hit him harder now. Pelting from every angle and also straight up from the ground. He felt slowed by it, slowed and assaulted, as if each raindrop were a separate obstacle. Reaching home, he went inside, took off his great coat and hat and set them upon the fine wooden rack that they had brought with them from London. Shaking out his beard and hair, he ran his fingers through them. Then he held his hands up to his mouth and breathed into his open palms. The warm air hovered there, but only for a second, and soon his skin was cold again. He breathed again, felt warm for several seconds and then cold again, warm and then cold. Cold. He dropped his hands down to his sides, thrust them into his pockets and sighed a silty, grainy sigh. One that seemed to come from the bottom of his soul's ocean. But then everything changed. His mood rocked and swayed, and Yochanan felt a smile flutter to his lips.

Laughing out loud, he turned and looked at his image in the gilt hall mirror. My, how shaggy! Wet! How disheveled! But happy! Happy! He found himself possessed of an excited and yet cautious confusion.

He had taken great pleasure outside the baker's door and yet there were so many sins and so much shame growing on the fields where this kind of pleasure bloomed. Where was his anger? He could not feel it now. Where was his litany, his sour prayer, his anger? Putting his hands over his face he pulled back on his own scalp, up from his forehead, feeling the prick and pull of each hair being stretched back and some even breaking. Yochanan loved his wife, and trusted her, too. Strangely, he still trusted her. The image of Esther in the baker's arms was an excruciatingly beautiful flower. Vicarious, criminal, devastating, and yet thrillful. He ached with every petal, leaf, and fresh-cut stem of it.

Once again, he imagined the baker's dark hands thrusting upward into Esther's body, her mouth half open, lips wet. Yochanan imagined and imagined, and grew once again aroused while standing alone in the antechamber, still dripping from the rain. But he didn't touch himself this time. He was in his own house and the walls were lined with holy books. Yochanan could not bring such odd, illicit flowers home with him. Here they wouldn't be fragrant, but sacrilegious, most foul.

Rubbing his hands together, he put them once more through his beard and hair. As if he could comb out the confusion. A servant walked into the antechamber.

"Oh Sir, I didn't hear you—come in, sit by the fire, take off your wet clothes, and eat some fresh rolls, just come from the baker, Esther, the Lady, your wife, she has just brought them, in through the kitchen courtyard door."

My father writes:
In 1837 there was a horrible earthquake in the northern mystical city of Sefat... Over five thousand people were killed, and those that escaped left the city and wandered throughout Palestine. Many half-mad old Kabbalists made their way to Jerusalem. The streets were full of their ragged and deranged numbers. Yochanan and Esther, working with the British Consul, set up a charitable foundation to aid their cause. Amongst other projects, they raised money for an orphanage. Once the money was raised, Esther became its defacto director.

I write:
While her husband had come in wet, Esther arrived home soaking. She had gotten caught in the brunt of the squall. And although both her color and her spirits were still lifted from her

doughy tryst, everything else about her dragged. Her hair had come loose under her hat and was lying in sopping tendrils all about her face. And her long maroon cloak, drenched on the bottom, dragged around her feet.

She threw off her floppy hat and stepped out of the cloak, gratefully peeling its wetness off of her body. The only dry thing about her were the rolls which were curled into a cloth that she had stuffed under her cloak and which she had held tight into her chest as she made her way home. Suddenly laughing, she thrust the rolls away from her body and into the hands of the servant who laughed along with her for no reason at all. They continued laughing, Esther and the servant girl, as Esther unconsciously ran her hands up and down her bodice. Her nipples were cold and hard. And they stung a bit, too. Esther dropped her hands and walked out of the kitchen, into the hallway on her way upstairs to change into dry clothes for dinner.

When she saw Yochanan standing in the front vestibule she stopped. His look was neither vacant of affection nor full of any familiar warmth. He was in between something and she knew not what but did have a frightful idea. She knew not how to respond. Again, she tried to smile. And this time was successful. But the smile brought another shiver. As if there were a bit of cold contained in the subtle upturn of her own lips which, with her smile, spilled out over her whole body. She hugged her arms about her. And she needed to speak. It was odd to stand there not speaking.

"One of the Sefat men begged to be let into our house, out of..." she began.

"And so you let him; it's raining, of course you let him."

"I led him to our door but at the last second he..."

"Ran away. Yes, they always run away."

"My husband. You look tired."

"My wife. You are very wet. Go dry yourself. And then we

will eat. I smell the bread. It smells good."

Esther walked towards her husband and continued to speak, "But just as I opened the door, the man ran from me." She stopped in front of her husband and held out her hand to touch his. Yochanan felt how cold she was. Esther spoke again, "The baker put in an extra roll. He is a good baker."

"My wife. Esther. You are very wet. Go upstairs, dry your—"

"My husband, I am going."

Yochanan watched after her as she climbed the stairs and rounded the landing. And as Esther disappeared from his view he felt that he could hear his own heart and smell his own blood and even feel his skin encasing his face and fingers, his legs and feet, his toes too. He felt taut and uncomfortable inside of himself. As if he were more a creaky machine than man, more a sum of mismatched parts than any sort of ethereal spirit. Whereas usually he felt the opposite. So comfortable with the feel of his own soul. And so familiar with it.

But now was not a time for soul. Actually, he couldn't feel his soul at all. Only his bones, and his body and all the blood running through it. Looking up the stairs again, he saw only emptiness. Then the green spot at the top of the hall snared his eyes; it was the picture, a landscape that his father had sent them, a present from Sheinlanka. Sent with the messenger whose eyes rolled this way and that, and in whom Esther had recognized a distant cousin's husband's younger brother or at least the form of someone remote and inconsequential whom she had once known.

"Well maybe not you," she had said when the messenger protested, "but definitely someone like you or at least like your face." Then all three—Yochanan, Esther, and the messenger—laughed at her rather silly if not poetic persistence.

"At least like your face." Now Yochanan mouthed his wife's words to himself, "At least like your face." The words didn't mean anything, but he felt an odd and pressing need to repeat them. As if this one fragment of nonsense could save him from having to live in a kind of wholeness that made too much sense. For the moment was whole. And he knew that he would not mention what he had seen to his wife but that she knew that he knew and that this was to be their secret. And he also knew that the secret would become, over time, a mistress to both of them, or rather, his mistress and her mister, a hermaphroditic silence that they would share and bed and ultimately believe in. For what is a secret, he painfully mused, but a kind of religion that leads the silent to constantly pray.

Focusing on the picture at the top of the stairs, he ran his fingers through his hair again, pulling each follicle upward from his scalp. And then he lowered his hand to his teeth and gently bit the knuckles. The skin gathered up like soft leather in his mouth. He pulled and then sucked, unconscious of the action but fully immersed in it. Meanwhile, watching quietly from the kitchen, the servant thought her master most strange.

My father writes:
Yochanan's father, the chief assistant of the Chatam Sofer, was the blind Rabbi Mordechai Schine. A legend has been passed down that his students never knew he was blind. According to the legend, Rabbi Mordechai Schine tricked his students into thinking that he could see by listening for the turning of pages as they studied the Talmud and following the text in his head. He must have known the entire Talmud by heart.

I write:
Esther changed quickly out of her wet clothes and came down for dinner. They ate in relative silence, whereas usually both chatted comfortably about their days. Then right after they had finished eating, the couple went up to their room and got into bed. It was much earlier than usual, but neither knew what else to do.

Esther was pious in her own way. She knew how to keep the

NOMI EVE

Sabbath holy but in private she often broke the rules. Yochanan
was pious but in a serious way. He knew the mitzvot and he
always kept the Sabbath holy. To him, creativity could come
only as a consequence of prayer and piety, not as a shaper of it.
Esther and Yochanan lay in their beds, side by side, barely any
space between them. As it was not her time of the month, the
beds were pushed together. On the days when she was bleeding
they would be pulled far apart. Esther fidgeted and couldn't lie
still. She sat halfway up and flipped her pillow over, fluffed it up,
and then rested her face into the cool linen. She watched
Yochanan's back. He was turned away from her, facing the
window on the east wall which looked out over the Mary
Church and farther in the distance also faced the garden the
Christians call Gethsemane, after the olive trees that grow there,
crooked and squat.

Esther sat up again and turned the pillow another time. But the
linen on the underside wasn't cool yet and this made her fidget
some more. She did not know what or how or how much he
knew, but she knew that Yochanan knew something. And
Esther wondered how this something fit into his prayers, let
alone into his pants. He was a most prayerful man, her husband,
from a long line of Rabbis reaching all the way back to Rashi,
the great eleventh-century commentator.

Shutting her eyes, Esther tried to sleep but she could not. She
kept seeing images and having odd thoughts and memories. She
felt filled with them. Her whole body dreaming, remembering,
thinking. One image would not leave her alone. It was of
Yochanan's father. She could not stop thinking about Yochanan's
father, a man whom she had never met, but whose story
fascinated her. Esther had a picture in her head of an old man
sitting at a table in the House of Study. He was surrounded by
many students and many books.

The image dissipated, leaving her alone with Yochanan in the
almost-dark. Esther closed her eyes and listened to her husband

breathing. Heavy and deep were his inhalations, and every couple of breaths a restless comma of a cough inserted itself into his repose. Sighing, Esther feared that he had caught cold in the rain. She rubbed her eyes and took a finger up to her right nipple which was still tender. The baker had taken her nipples into his mouth and sucked them until she felt like screaming in pleasure but she hadn't screamed, instead she turned the yell inward as she had taught herself to do, inviting it into an inner cavern where voices were always echoing and the trick was never to try to contain them but just to let them joyously be. She moved her hand off of her breast and traveled it down in between her legs, but only for a second. Not for pleasure, but for the comfortable and warmclose feeling of touching herself. And then she curled over on her side and shut her eyes.

She pretended that every time Yochanan inhaled was the turning of a page and every time he exhaled was the ending of a chapter. In this way, she read the Talmud of their togetherness. It was a big book. A book that contained all that had already passed between them as well as all that would ever pass between them. Past and present and future all were written there. She read for a long time, so many shared stories, some intimate, some silly, others dark and uncomfortable, some so beloved that she almost cried from them.

The night passed heavily. No, thought Esther, Jerusalem is not a place for regular sleep. Only for a kind of restless snuggling inward that leaves a soul dreamily awake all day long. Yochanan slept deeply; his breath was a parchment of air which she read from for a long time. And then, as the sky lightened, Esther moved towards her husband and roused him gently. Yochanan wrapped his arms around her and nuzzled his lips into her hair. She pressed her body into his, and together they slept, adding another page there.

Siobhan Dowd, program director of PEN American Center's Freedom-to-Write Committee, writes this column regularly, alerting readers to the plight of writers around the world who deserve our awareness and our writing action.

Writer Detained: Wei Jingsheng
by Siobhan Dowd

*W*ei Jingsheng has had many things said of him in his turbulent career as a Chinese dissident. He has been called mad, mischievous, and moderate—a spy, a subversive, and a conspirator. He himself is the first to acknowledge that he is not always the easiest person to know. "I was always a troublemaker," he recalled once in an interview, "even as a kid." A Nobel Peace Prize nominee, Wei is often dubbed the Nelson Mandela of China. He has already served fourteen years in prison for his outspoken opposition to his government. Today he is back in jail, set to serve another fourteen years, for alleged sedition.

Wei Jingsheng

Born in 1950 in Chao County, Anhui Province, Wei is the son of a high-ranking army officer. One of his baby pictures shows him in the arms of Jiiang Qing, Mao's wife. He was brought up on a diet of political thought. Both his mother and father, he recalls, were against children reading novels, and he had to make do with the memoirs of early

Glimmer Train Stories, Issue 19, Summer 1996
©1996 Siobhan Dowd

Communist Party leaders. He joined the Red Guards at the age of sixteen, a time when he described himself as fanatically Maoist. "I saw that all the inequality and unhappiness of our society had been brought about by these class enemies who had wormed their way into the Party. Whereupon I threw myself wholeheartedly into the campaign to ferret out such creatures." Soon, however, he became confused. In a brilliant memoir of the period, he describes how he boarded a train and set out west toward Xian, so that by surveying the countryside he might learn more. There were beggars everywhere, but when he tried to offer food to them, other passengers reprimanded him, saying that the beggars were "probably bad class elements, former landlords or rich peasants." Later in his travels he came upon demobilized soldiers with nothing to do, impoverished village communities, a woman covered only in mud and ashes—in short, a nation in chaos. "From this time onwards, whenever I read of 'the superiority of socialism over capitalism,' I would dismiss it as so much bullshit. The capitalism I had read about in books may have been terrible, but I couldn't believe that there was anything worse about it than the things I had seen on my travels."

He concluded that the Cultural Revolution had not worked. "We, the top Peking cadres' kids," he explained later, "were the first ones into the Red Guards and the first ones to get disillusioned." Thus, by the age of seventeen, Wei's carefully indoctrinated revolutionary beliefs had themselves been revolutionized. Over the next twelve years he trained as an electrician, found work in Beijing's zoo, and voraciously read everything he could find. He first came to prominence in the Democracy Wall movement of 1978.

On December 15 of that year, Wei posted a long article entitled "The Fifth Modernization." Crowds gathered to read it, so audacious was it in tone. A group of young men was inspired by it to visit the author, and, after a long night of heated discussion on Hegel, Marx, and other political theorists, the young men decided to found a new magazine, *Exploration*. The first issue consisted of three articles, all by Wei; copies of the new magazine were distributed at the Democracy Wall. By issue three, printed on March 11, 1979, the print run was eight hundred. Eighteen days later, Wei was arrested. The Democracy Wall was shut down soon afterward and all those foremost in posting materials on it were silenced, either by intimidation or, like Wei, by imprisonment. The brief movement had died.

Wei was sentenced to fifteen years imprisonment at a trial the following October. His defense speech berated the leadership in no uncertain terms:

> The leaders of our nation must be informed that we want to take our destiny into our own hands. We want no more gods and emperors. No more saviours of any kind. We want to be masters of our own country.

Wei served all but a few months of his sentence. During his incarceration, he lost nearly half his teeth, was beaten several times, and spent long periods in virtual isolation. This punishment, he observed, was the worst. "Isolation," he said, "was being left to punish yourself." He released his fiancée from their engagement and said what saved him from despair was not having a family dependent upon him.

On being released, he lived life in freedom to the full; he frequented bars and nightclubs, drank copious beers, and only stopped short of dancing and singing because, he said, he had fallen behind the times. On the intellectual front, he published articles in newspapers abroad, including the *New York Times,* and gave interviews to foreign reporters elucidating his views and describing China's ongoing repression of its citizens in graphic detail. His view on China's bid to host the 2000 Olympics was not the predictable one. "I supported China's bid," he wrote, "however, I am thoroughly against the use of force to suppress those opposed to the bid." When the U.S. Assistant Secretary of

State for Human Rights and Humanitarian Affairs, John Shattuck, visited China, Wei had a long discussion with him.

None of these activities went unnoticed. On March 5, 1994, officer Zhang Shichao of the Beijing Public Security Bureau took Wei on another "tour" of the country. When Wei insisted on being brought back to Beijing, he was ferried as far as a suburb, transferred to a police car, and taken away. A search of his apartment followed on April 5. The government described him as being under "residential surveillance." On November 21, 1995, he was formally accused of attempting to overthrow the government. On December 13, he received his fourteen-year sentence. If he serves his sentence in full, he will be almost sixty and will have spent almost half his life behind bars. Two days after he was sentenced, his sister Wei Shan-Shan, addressing a press conference hosted by PEN in New York, commented, "This time, even though he has done nothing, the Chinese government has sentenced him again, very heavily. I believe they have done this because he is a prominent name and, by punishing this famous person, they are sending a test to the international community to see how much we care about the injustice."

Letters appealing for Wei's release can be sent to:

> LI PENG, PREMIER
> GUOWUYAN
> 9 XIHAUNGCHENGGENBEIJIE
> BEIJING 100032
> PEOPLE'S REPUBLIC OF CHINA

or faxed to 011 8610 467 7351.

Letters should begin with this salutation: *Your Excellency.*

Lara Stapleton

*This photo reveals things about us as children which I believe
still hold true to this day: my brother with that distracted
amusement, my sister, shy, concentrating—me, trying very
hard with that little chest thrown out. Our nightgowns were
blood red and my sister's hair the richest black. That's my
pop. Ma was taking the picture.*

Lara Stapleton's work has been published in the *Chattahoochee Review,* the
Alaska Quarterly Review, Another Chicago Magazine, the *Michigan Quarterly
Review, Columbia,* and the *Asian-Pacific American Journal.* She has recently
completed a collection, *The Next Place,* and is at work on the novel *The Lowest
Blue Flame Before Nothing,* of which this is an excerpt.

Born and raised in Michigan, Stapleton currently resides in New York City.
She is a graduate of NYU's writing program and teaches at Long Island
University in Brooklyn, and Pratt Institute.

LARA STAPLETON

The Lowest Blue Flame Before Nothing

Lourdes and Luz would have a field day with the weight categories. Light-on-the-heavy-side-not-too-much-mayo weight. Isty-bitsy-teeny-weeny weight. Fly-in-the-buttermilk weight. Fly-in-the-face-of-convention weight. Baton weight. Bataan weight. Needle-in-a-haystack weight. Not-at-all weight. Sneeze weight. Lourdes, whose sophomore algebra was fresh in her memory, observed that light heavyweight must be like $X+ -X$, and means you weigh zero, and that must be the lightest category of all. They went on into equations. What is junior-dust-under-the-couch weight minus wet-towel weight? *That's negative, clearly,* Luz said. *Okay,* Lourdes said, *Miss Know It All—toe-nail-clipping weight by passing-wind. Disgusting,* Luz said, and then they stopped, grinning. They bordered on ruining it by going on too long.

And later again, Lourdes would say that that was the turning point. Lourdes would say that that was the day which destroyed Dulce. They had lost her once and for all. Luz, who was the eldest and held greater strength of conviction, would say that it was just a coincidence, that that day, the day Dulce met Zuke the boxer, was only a normal teenage act of rebellion. She would argue that she herself had done the same thing, at thirteen, the night she drank three beers at Maria Luna Saguid's house. *Testing limits,* Luz said. *You, Lourdes,* she said, *for a week straight you skipped ballet and made out with the Impala. Where did he get that damn Impala? I never made out with him,* Lourdes said, *we only drove around and held hands, and they had money because his father had been a diplomat.*

Lourdes begged to differ. Lourdes, who knew deep down inside that she was right, but had trouble arguing with her elder sister, said that the day they met Zuke was a foreshadowing. A clear sign of things to come, and if they, the women—the two older and wiser sisters and their mother—if they had knocked some sense into Dulce back then the later tragedy would have never arisen.

No, Luz said, *the first time was normal; later, it was crazy.* Later, they had already lost her.

Beg-to-differ weight. Shadow-on-a-cloudy-day.

Dulce: she woke that morning into a stillness all her own. Before she even opened her eyes there was a mint flavor, and her breathing stung slightly, a good cold sting, balm. From the moment she woke she longed to be outside so her skin could drink the sun. She was euphoric. She was fifteen. She sat for a moment on the edge of the bed and blinked the sleep from her eyes. Lourdes lay in the twin bed across the room. They would be going to a fair that day. The three sisters would go to the International Festival at the park.

For Lourdes, that day had been something else entirely. What she tasted was not something you're supposed to taste. Slightly poison. Like not getting the last bit of paint off your hands, or soap. She knew from the start that it would simply be a day to get through. She couldn't lay her finger on it but it was everything. She *heard* the morning noises of the house—the pipes with their refusal of rhythm, her father urinating in the bathroom, the obscene swallow of the toilet. Her scalp itched. Her white bras were all dingy and full of lint. There was

Glimmer Train Stories

certainly a pea in the mattress, boy.

Lourdes tried to keep it to herself, noticing that Dulce was ecstatic, that Dulce carried the expression of a child about to break into run. Lourdes knew instinctively that Luz and Dulce would not tolerate her foul mood, would mock and further irritate her. And so she was silent. And so she didn't complain when Dulce turned the radio to a station that didn't come in clearly, letting that static burn and sizzle through to ruin a beautiful song.

Dulce with her incomprehensible outburst of affection. She kissed her parents and sisters. She grabbed their hands and danced while the others were still staring with weariness.

Dulce pinched her shoulder blades back and put on her most womanly dress. A bright yellow thing that fell just over her knees. She looked curvier.

She was indeed the curvy one. Dulce was thick and dark like her mother's side. Luz and Lourdes had the look of Chinese girls, slender and yellow, like their father. Dulce was the dark one. Her hair was just a bit coarse. For this reason she was their mother's baby, the island child.

Seemed Baning spent all those young years braiding Dulce's hair at the kitchen table. Braiding and unbraiding, braiding and unbraiding, toward an absurd perfection. The other two were jealous and watched huddled from the bottom of the stairs.

That day, Luz and Dulce couldn't stop touching each other and Lourdes walked briskly ahead. The two linked arms. They pressed their cheeks together. The three of them had been given two dollars apiece. They were to be home by nightfall.

Dulce imitated Lourdes's walk. She always walked like a dancer. Feet turned permanently out into second position. One arm squeezing a bulky bag against her side, one arm arranged with delicacy—that slightly extended pointer finger, that curve of the wrist. Luz whispered loudly enough to be overheard: "You think that maybe one day she would leave the house without her hair in a bun."

Dulce did her own big clunky imitation of a pirouette. Luz's was closer, being that she was slight-framed like a ballerina, being that her body worked that way. They asked did Lourdes want to go back and get her tutu.

The sun was raging, interrogating, but there was a breeze strong enough to bring relief, goose pimples. The wind lifted Dulce's skirt slightly and she liked it. Lourdes's skirt was a narrow fit and Luz's defied gravity and stayed put. Dulce turned her face up and opened her mouth, as if there were a sweet rain. Lourdes looked for shade. She would walk swiftly ahead with her out-turned feet and then pause to wait under an awning for the other two. And then she'd do it again.

Their mother had packed them a bag and Lourdes had it squeezed under an elbow. Baning had insisted on giving them six large pork buns, each wrapped in aluminum foil. There would be food at the fair, but Baning insisted. She gave them a thermos of Kool-Aid. Lourdes could hear it sloshing as she stepped. The bag was bulky enough that when Lourdes turned sideways she was not conscious of her girth. They stopped in a little deli for candy, and things behind Lourdes got knocked off the shelves and when she turned to eye the tumbling cans, boxes fell. Luz and Dulce snorted into their fists.

Lourdes reminded herself that sometimes you feel like this. That sometimes you have moods where little things mean more than they would on other days. Her headache was a barely perceptible hum, the lowest blue flame before nothing. She wanted to grab Luz by the hair—not Dulce, but Luz. Luz could so easily gather Dulce against Lourdes, when for the most part she didn't care. It was Dulce and Lourdes who shared a room. Lourdes who spooned Dulce when she cried.

Lourdes was seventeen and Luz was one year older.

Lourdes grew increasingly resentful that she was burdened with the heavy bag while the other two skipped and fell over each other. "You take it," she said, holding it at arm's length to Luz. Luz said, "No way, José," and then Lourdes looked to Dulce. She would have said please to Dulce, but Dulce looked to Luz.

Lourdes grumbled. There was the sloshing of the Kool-Aid and the embarrassing scent of the pork. She was a block ahead of the other two anyway when she paused to open the thermos. "Do you want any?" she asked with a seriousness that made the other two giggle. Luz shook her head with a choreographed stiffness. Lourdes poured the sugary purple slowly on the edge of the sidewalk as she walked. She tried to match the stream with the crack. When she was done, she threw the pork buns back at her sisters—the aluminum foil was hot by now, and they threw a couple back again and Lourdes didn't laugh but she sighed.

By the time they entered the park, the three were walking together. It was overwhelmingly crowded. Luz said it was a fire hazard. It was like registration, she told Lourdes, who would be registering for the first time that fall.

Lourdes wanted to go home immediately. It stunk in that gross human way. Dulce said they should go back and get the pork buns off the sidewalk and sell them for a dime apiece. Luz said it would be a nickel to lick the Kool-Aid off the cement. They bought lemonades and intricate clay dragons on sticks from a Chinese lady. Most of their money was gone. They ran into their mother's best friend's daughter and walked with her a while until she took off with her boyfriend. A white girl wasn't looking and almost dropped her ice cream on Dulce. Dulce cursed her with the dragon and then imitated. They stood next to a bench, waiting for a mother to take her children and leave. Dulce called them brats and waved her monster on a stick when the woman wasn't looking. The lady finally got up and the girls collapsed against each other and fanned pamphlets over their faces.

There were boys on fences. There were boys on fences all over the park. In pairs and threesomes and ten at a time. Lourdes and

Luz weren't particularly fond of these young men, but Dulce, she couldn't help herself. Dulce had lingered a few steps behind whenever her sisters got distracted. Her spine curved up. She smiled back at the hissing, calling boys, and then ran with her

secret naughtiness back in step with the other two.

There were two particular boys not far from where the sisters fell into each other on the bench. They were facing them from the other side of the fountain. The fountain blocked half of the tall, skinny one, but his friend was clearly in view. One was tall and skinny with glasses, clearly a sissy, and the other was short and also thin but very muscular. The short one wore a T-shirt fit to burst and a loose pair of chinos. He had a lot of energy. He hopped up on the fence and then down, up on the fence and then down. He gesticulated to his friend and turned to watch girls pass this way and that. The tall one stayed on the fence. They were Mexicans. The short one had a buzz cut and a thick, vague face. The tall one's bangs rolled over in front and were greasy.

It was obvious that the short one would do the talking. They were the kind of friends where the one would do the talking while the other one stuffed his fists in his pockets, shrugged his shoulders, and hovered awkwardly. The tall one would stand back a bit and nod at what the other one said and blush when the short one embarrassed him.

Dulce liked the short one. He had big, rich, brown eyes, darker than his hair. His eyes were big enough that she could see them from her side of the fountain. She liked the way he made fists loosely at his side, how quickly he turned from one direction to another.

The short one said something that made three girls laugh. Three Mexican girls suddenly bent a bit and one with a ponytail looked back. The girls kept walking and the short boy turned to his friend on the fence and raised his hands for a little victory pose. Dulce kept watching until he glanced in her direction and then she looked quickly away.

He called across to her in Spanish. Dulce looked one way and then the other to make sure it was meant for her. "What?" she called back, scooching forward and upsetting the way her sisters were balanced against her. He called again and she yelled back that she didn't speak Spanish. Luz and Lourdes looked to each other. He called back in English, and asked her her name. Luz yelled, "She doesn't speak English," and broke herself up, but Dulce yelled, "Dulce," and grinned.

The new friend turned for a moment to conference with the tall one. Everything that short one did was exaggerated. When he nodded it was to be seen for blocks, the same as when he shrugged or waved his hand in disagreement.

"What the hell are you doing?" Lourdes said through her teeth, but Dulce sat where she was scooched, waiting, and ignored her.

The tall one got off the fence and arranged himself against it. He leaned where he had been sitting, with his elbows slung back and one foot crossed over the other. The short one gestured to Dulce, come here, come here, with big arcs of his hand, and Dulce stood and smoothed her skirt over her ass.

"What the hell are you doing?" Lourdes said again, but Dulce sashayed away.

Luz looked to Lourdes. "We shouldn't let her go by herself."

"We shouldn't let her go at all."

"So go grab her by the scruff of the neck."

"Go with her."

"You go talk to those hoodlums."

They watched for a moment as Dulce swayed back and forth like a four-year-old with her thumb in her mouth. Then they went to slowly join her. As they got closer, it became apparent that something was very wrong with the short one's face. It was thickened and leathery and his nose was on crooked. His eyes were fine, but just the eyes, not the lids. The lids were as puffy as an old man's. It was like a doe behind a mask.

"I was just telling Dulce here," the boy told the older sisters, "I used to know some Filipinos and they was good people."

Luz and Lourdes stood close enough together and far enough away to speak under their breath without being heard by the others.

"And then you killed them?" Luz whispered, but she nodded appreciatively.

"He ate them like the Jolly Green Giant." This was Lourdes.

"The Jolly Brown Dwarf."

Zuke was indeed a very small person. Smaller than Dulce, certainly, who stood out in the middle, giggling an octave higher than her sisters had ever heard, with her butt up in the air. Dulce with her thick calves, her solid limbs. The boy was just as short and downright skinny but with these muscles tacked on. His arms swelled out at the biceps, a snake with prey in its endless throat.

"My name is Zuke." He put his hand to the side of his mouth like he was calling across a canyon, mocking Lourdes and Luz for standing so far away. "This is my cousin, Rudy." He pointed to the tall one who rearranged himself against the fence.

Luz nodded like peace-be-with-you, a few pews away, as if hands were too far for grasping, an enforced friendliness. Lourdes smiled but her top lip inched up in the middle. They didn't return his gesture. They didn't mention their names.

"Those are my sisters," Dulce said, this too with bubbles. "Lourdes and Luz," and Zuke said he never would have guessed, no, for real, that the two looked alike, but not Dulce.

There came a moment of silence. There came a moment of heat, no wind to break that unforgiving sun. Rudy pulled his shirt away from his armpits and readjusted his glasses.

"Gee, it's hot," Dulce gushed, waving the bottom of her yellow dress around.

"Yeah," Zuke said. "I have to be careful, with the heat, you know. I have to be careful with my health, 'cuz I'm a athlete. I'm a boxer, ya know."

Dulce visibly gasped. She bounced up on her heels. You would have sworn she'd clap her hands goodie.

"Yeah, I'm a bantamweight. Rudy here, he's a junior welterweight, but he don't fight so that's okay. What are you?" he asked Dulce.

Dulce: I don't know, *gush, gush, giggle giggle.*

He: You look like a——, *he looks her up and down. The sisters lean forward first with their mouths open in disbelief and then quickly, they sneer,* ——maybe a featherweight. No offense, but that's more than me.

She: *puts her hands on her hips in mock anger and then runs the scales in laughter.*

He: Or maybe a junior. Let's see——, *he walks toward her with his arms spread, as if he's going to grab her by the middle and lift.*

The sisters moved forward. The sisters, linked at the arm as one unit, took a step in, and Zuke must have seen it out of the corner of his eye, because he did not pick up Dulce by the middle. Dulce swayed this way and that.

Lourdes wanted to mash that mashed face. "We should go home," she called to Dulce, who ignored her.

"Look," Zuke said. "I'll teach you—heavyweight, cruiserweight, light heavyweight, supermiddleweight ..." Dulce repeated and uncurled a finger for each category.

The breeze disappeared again. The sun made them moist, made them all squint and shade their eyes at once. Luz took a handkerchief from Lourdes's bag and mopped her brow.

Lourdes fell to dreaming, awake, in the heat. In the dream she was dancing. There was a recital during which she got a cramp. It was the kind of thing, had it been in class, the instructor would have run to her with concern, or the girl next to her would have known, would have grabbed Lourdes's calf and started kneading because they all know what it feels like when your muscles betray you. When that long, thin muscle becomes a dense sphere, a filled rubber ball, an anvil.

But it was a recital. If you had looked closely, if you had known what you were looking for, you could have seen it, one smooth, curving muscle and one sudden, relentless round fruit.

54   *Glimmer Train Stories*

Lourdes finished. She flexed her foot once but that was her only attempt at relief, her only break. It was a minute or two. She completed the *pas de beret,* the turn section, and the *grand jeté.* She finished on one knee. And when it was over she sobbed backstage, and clutched first her friend Angie, and then Miss Ruth, as they rubbed the stubborn mass back from pain.

"How long was it like this?" Angie asked, and Lourdes said the last half, and Angie said Lourdes was a heroine. They were still clapping out front and it was Lourdes's glory and Miss Ruth told not only Lourdes's class, but all the classes except the littlest girls, who might have been frightened, how very brave Lourdes had been.

Luz put her chin on Lourdes's shoulder and woke the younger from her musings. Luz looked for Lourdes's eyes so they could stand in judgment together. Zuke was shadowboxing. Zuke was a hero too. He said, "Ima buy a Lamborghini. Pow. Boom. Ima buy my mother a fur coat. Pow. Pow. Whatchyou want, Grandma? Whatchyou want, Sinbad?" Aside: "That's my trainer." Dulce fluttered. "Whatchyou want, Dulce?" He winked at her and paused, posing with his fists up. "Huh? What you want? Channel Number Five? Shoes?"

Luz and Lourdes had had enough, and instinctively moved together to take their sister lightly by the elbow. Dulce shook them off. Zuke went on: he told Dulce how there was a fighter, he was famous; you never heard of him? He's Puerto Rican— his wife had a shoe collection and she would put sequins on them. That was what she liked to do, glue those little sparkly things ...

Rudy had been staring off somewhere else for a long time. He seemed an ally to the older girls. The whole thing made him uncomfortable. Luz and Lourdes each took an arm and tried to gently turn their sister, the grief-stricken mother at the coffin. She didn't know her own mind and should be treated gently yet firmly. Dulce yanked her arms from their touchings.

The breeze came back, stronger yet, lifting Dulce's hair in the wind to black flames, her skirt. They all shivered. Zuke looked down at Dulce's legs. Lourdes bore her teeth. "Dulce, it is time for us to go home right now."

Dulce looked at her watch, said no it's not, and made it clear that her sister was lying. Zuke started talking faster. He seemed to feel that if no one else could get a word in edgewise, they wouldn't be able to end the conversation. The girls stepped back and he stepped forward, reaching out and over with that babble, *One time there was a fighter and that guy was already twenty-three and Zuke himself is only seventeen and he annihilated that old man, how old are you Dulce...?* but he talked right over her answer, *let me guess, oh, I'm right—I figured. You could be older, though, you got that sophisticated look, but I guessed ...* There was something panicked in his talking and it gave both Luz and Lourdes the creeps.

Lourdes made Dulce turn to her. She didn't care if it was rude. "We are going home."

"No."

And then Zuke said, "Let me buy y'all some Italian ice. You girls want some Italian ice," and Lourdes said, "No, we're going home."

Dulce set her jaw. "Excuse me one second, Zuke," she said, with her shoulders up around her ears, and her spine, curling, curling. She, Dulce, that little girl, grabbed her sisters by the elbows and pulled them aside.

"I am going to get some Italian ice. I don't care what you do."

"No."

"How are you going to stop me?"

"I'll beat you right here, I swear to God." This was Lourdes.

"Go ahead."

"Dulce, are you crazy? Look at him." This was Lourdes again. Dulce looked over and gushed. "He looks like an assassin."

"He's ugly," Luz said.

Dulce's head was shaking, something Lourdes had never seen before. She had never seen Dulce so stubborn. She would not admit the possibility of anything else.

"Beat me."

"Ma will beat you when you get home."

"What are you going to tell her? I had Italian ice? She's going to beat me for Italian ice?"

"I *will* tell her." This was still Lourdes, and even Luz was shocked by the proposal of tattling; they were way beyond the years of tattling.

"Do what you want. Go home and tell Ma, or beat me right here, *like you could,* but I am going to get Italian ice with Zuke. You can come if you want." She walked back to rejoin he who was now her date.

Lourdes's eyes darted all over Luz's face. Luz should have done something. Luz was the oldest. Dulce would have listened to Luz. "We have to go with her," Lourdes said. She was about to cry. Luz scrunched up her eyes with more accusation of insanity. Lourdes's desperation was more ridiculous than the whole ridiculous situation. Too much passion for this dumb day.

Luz thought of who might see her. She thought of a boy she liked from last year's biology and she thought of Jenny who was always looking for a good reason to say horrible things. Luz did not want to be seen with that ugly hoodlum. They argued, but it didn't matter. Dulce went for the ice.

"It's just over there," she called as she walked with Zuke and Rudy. It made Lourdes feel better that Rudy went too, and she could see the cart from where they stood.

Zuke didn't touch her. He turned back to wave at Dulce's sisters.

And it wasn't very long that Lourdes took her eyes off of Dulce. It was just long enough to threaten Luz with telling their mother, and complain that Luz could have stopped the whole thing, and long enough for Luz to say Lourdes was a big baby and that everyone was acting crazy. It couldn't have been more than a moment, but there was Rudy, the embarrassed messenger, talking without looking up, his black glasses sliding down his damp face. "Your sister said she'll be home before dark." And Dulce was nowhere in sight.

The breeze disappeared.

The seething sun.

Lourdes took the leadership as she and Luz searched, shading their eyes. This was the first time Luz didn't behave as the eldest; it had been stripped of her. Lourdes just walked where she would, knowing Luz would fall in beside her. Knowing Luz should have done right earlier if she was going to do right. They combed the park. They chased a yellow dress, and it was a Filipino girl too, until the wrong gesture cleared things up. You would know from a distance, even, your sister's vocabulary of gesture. You would know her pacing. They saw Rudy again, shuffling with his fists in his pockets, and he promised to look too, to tell Dulce to wait by the fountain, but Lourdes didn't believe him. They saw a kid or two from the neighborhood, but no one had seen a sign. Lourdes walked around front of a group, to get a look at a short Mexican in chinos and a T-shirt. She walked to look him full in the face, and the guy's girlfriend asked her what the hell she was doing. She kept moving. They split up and met back at the fountain and then Luz said, "Look, we have to go home, if she gets home before us we'll really be in for it."

Luz said, "We'll tell Ma she went off with Linda," their mom's best friend's daughter, "and we'll call Linda and tell her what to say, too." "No way, José," Lourdes said. "I am going to tell Ma the truth. I don't care what you say. Dulce can't act like this. She has to learn."

They walked home with their defiant jaws. Nervous, and mad at each other. Lourdes's headache pulsed. She had to stop and close her eyes to cool it. They walked by the Chinese-food place, where an *n* had fallen off so that the sign read *Chinatow*. Luz nudged Lourdes to point it out and Lourdes said, "So what." Then Luz said, "Light-on-the-heavy-side-not-too-much-mayo weight, itsy-bitsy-teeny-weeny weight." And Lourdes couldn't resist and said, "Fly-in-the-buttermilk weight, fly-in-the-face-of-convention." And then she laughed so hard she forgot her heated brain, until they got very close to home and grew at first quiet, and then argued again about what to tell their mother.

Lourdes with her *poise.* Her placing one foot then the other on the stoop, the stairs. The toe before the heel. The precision of her fingers on the banister, the doorknob, her nimble, darting fingers. Everything always placed, never put. Lourdes looked very much like Luz, a version wound up taller with posture, but Lourdes's eyes were all her own. Nothing like the rest of her family, with their eyes open and *receiving,* their come-what-may eyes. Lourdes's eyes were always planning, narrowing, focused, her brow furrowed.

Luz knocked. Lourdes's stomach surged. They would all be in trouble, but she would take responsibility. Lourdes prepared herself. She stood up, up. Baning answered the door and smiled. The two came in and Baning looked out in the hallway for the third. Before she could ask, Lourdes blurted, "Ma, Dulce went to get Italian ice with a boy she just met and never came back."

Baning's expression twisted. This would have to be repeated.

Luz said, "Oh, Ma, she just went with Linda and Linda's boyfriend and a friend of Linda's boyfriend. They promised to be home before dark."

Lourdes felt she had been generous because she did not say that the boy was a mash-faced Mexican boxer. Now, if she told, she would make two of them liars. It would be two against one, and Luz and Dulce who would be not speaking to her. Dulce with her broad back turned, with silence to Lourdes's stories. Luz should be the wise one. Luz should know right and save Dulce. Lourdes looked to her sister whose expression of defiance was only meant for her. Luz's face was so subtle Baning would never see. Luz would make Lourdes look crazy to save her own ass.

Baning sighed and said nothing. Luz went to the corner store to call Linda from a public phone and then waited on the stoop for Dulce as long as she could, until their mother called dinner. Lourdes clutched a pillow in her bedroom, plotting how to teach Dulce. None of her ideas would take hold. Usually answers came to Lourdes and stayed. Usually she would think for a moment and she would know. But on this day, she would decide and then a moment later forget what the decision had been. She was malfunctioning, dizzy. She had to save Dulce, but. Luz was bullying her, but. The phone. The truth.

It was dusk when they ate. It was nearly dark. Usually Lourdes ate so neatly. Usually Lourdes was the one who cut small squares of her chicken, or only ate so many noodles and turned the fork over, back up, to place each small portion in her mouth and wipe with the napkin from her lap. She ate more than anybody and took her time doing so. But on this night she didn't eat. Lourdes basically stirred her food. And when the doorknob turned, Luz, thinking ahead, before Dulce even shut the door behind her, Luz, with her mouth full of noodles, said, "Did you have a nice time with Linda and her boyfriend and that friend of his?" with her stern, warning eyes. Baning said she was a bit late. Was she hungry? No, Dulce wasn't hungry, and she swooned past them into her bedroom and swooned onto her bed so that she could stare at the ceiling and swoon.

There is a certain way that aunts raise their nieces and nephews. They love them for their missing sister, the dead, ill, or indifferent. A double love. Love for a ghost and then some. Lourdes, years later, would raise Dulce's son with a bit of restrained madness, a desire to stave the disaster she could not stave before. She would be afraid to touch him. This, the fly-in-the-fist weight. Weight of the soul she did not save.

Writing out of Ireland: A Terrible Beauty Is Reborn
An essay by Annie Callan

Imagine this: a scenic, fertile island populated by artists, poets, writers, actors, musicians; a sympathetic government, which provides hefty subsidies and tax breaks to its creatively-inclined citizens; a resident poet-minister who supervises the ongoing health of the state's arts, culture, and native tongue; bountiful cafes, experimental theatres, galleries, underground spaces, and lofts teeming with performances. Heaven, right? Not quite. We're talking 1990s Ireland, that minuscule scrap of land on the outer fringes of Europe, which may be deep in the grip of another heady arts renaissance, but it depends on who you talk to.

Time was, and not so long ago, you'd mention Irish literature, and those spectral luminaries, Yeats, Shaw, Beckett, Wilde, Synge, would spring to mind. Although most of these brilliant scribes have been dead for nigh on half a century now, their cumulative genius helped situate this small island on the international literary map. Since then, succeeding writers have skulked uncertainly in their long shadow, or at least, until lately: today, there is such a proliferation of creative talent that one jaded cynic suggests issuing "an embargo against any more promising young writers."

On a visit home to my native Dublin last summer, however, it was hard not to get caught up in the electric spirit pervading the city. With a burgeoning film industry underway, big names were pouring in, and trendy nightclubs and bistros springing up to accommodate them. On the walls of Bono's brother's new restaurant hung autographed poems, for eventual auction, the proceeds of which would assist the continuing gentrification of the inner city, including the arts district, Temple Bar, Ireland's answer to Greenwich Village. Then there was the new Writers Museum to see, and the lunchtime plays at Bewley's Cafe.

The pedestrian Grafton Street throbbed with performers—a string quartet, a post-punk band, a fiddler, a mime troupe. At the tip of Stephen's Green, a middle-aged man stood ready to recite to you your favorite poem, for a minimal charge. Poetry is taken very seriously here. Ireland is one of the few countries where you'll find a poet advertising products on TV: the esteemed poet and professor-about-town, Brendan Kennelly, has a regular gig as Toyota's mouthpiece. The extent of his clout becomes readily apparent when you consider that he in fact never gets behind the wheel of a car: he walks everywhere (which, if you believe that the poet is spokesperson for the tribe, makes Kennelly a bit of a liar ...).

Books in general sell well here, poetry included. Where else do you find poetry collections on the best-seller list? Of course, the recent conferral of the world's most prestigious literary award, the Nobel Prize, on Irish poet Seamus Heaney hasn't hurt. Heaney, who was away in the Greek Isles at the time of the announcement, missed his own party, but, as with Irish wakes, the country forged ahead with its celebrations in the absence of its honored guest.

Dublin is not the only sultan of literary style. Paul Durcan, from County Mayo, is another popular poet, whose sweeping gestures and colorful declaratives make him a highly engaging reader. A sort of latterday Dylan Thomas, he is part actor, part ham, part prophet. To his credit, he started out by publishing his own books, and marketing himself, a task he embraced confidently, and today, he's one of the best-selling poets in the country. Saucy titles are often a seduction into the world of his poetics, such as "My Beloved Compares Herself to a Bottle of Stout" and "The Woman Who Keeps Her Breasts in the Back Garden."

Galway too is a bustling, west-coast arts community. Europeans have moved there in recent years, setting up exotic restaurants, and selling their wares—goats' cheese, yogurt, stuffed olives—at the Saturday market, just a book's toss away from Nora Barnacle's house, where Joyce came to meet his beloved's family. The highlight of the town for the bibliophile, though, is Kenny's bookstore. Nestled on a winding back street, it houses a bounty of books, its specialty being Irish writers. Des, the owner, will toss a selection of the newest into your lap, which, you can be sure, he has read and vetted for you. The walls are a gallery of photographs, signed by visiting celebrities.

To the north, Sligo, while still loyal to its native hero, Yeats (see: Yeats Football Club, and Yeat's Caife, a fast-food joint!), it now gathers writers from the world over for its literary festivals. The same may be said of almost every county in the country. Such is Ireland's formidable literary reputation today that Dublin has been chosen as the site of the new IMPAC literary prize, which will grant annually 100,000 pounds to a fiction writer (not necessarily from Ireland), one of the highest purses of its kind in the world.

But before you sell everything and make plans to emigrate, consider this: Almost one-fifth of Ireland's 3.5 million residents is unemployed; half of its population is under twenty-five; its authoritarian church wields immense power; petty crime is on the rise; and Dublin, for all its urbane appeal, is better known as the Heroin Capital of Europe. Given its torrid history of endless invasions, tribal wars, and economic vicissitudes, it's little surprise that Ireland is grappling frantically to come to terms with its newfound place in the spotlight. It is a nation experiencing growing pains. Despite its literary prowess, it is still struggling to wrest itself free from its complex past, this slightly schizo-phrenic, dark child of Europe. A country built on schisms, it is now dueling with itself. It has one foot firmly entrenched in centuries past, wanting to uphold its ancient traditions. But since the advent of television in the sixties, it has the other boot—or maybe it should be high heel—permanently pointed toward materialism.

With a dying language, Gaelic, and a twenty-year membership in the progressive European Union (of which it is head this year), Ireland wants the best of both worlds. Here is a place where ancient Viking sites have been ruthlessly paved over to make room for parking lots, and a place where the government might pay you to speak Irish—once the native tongue—in your home. How can this tiny nation embrace the modern world, where English is the common currency of communication, and still hold fast to those relics which make it special in the first place? What is it to be Irish today? Hordes of writers obsess about this in their fiction, so much so that some claim they are "bathed in their own self-regard."

If this is so, at least the focus is shifting away from the weight of their literary lineage. Many Irish writers have felt crippled by the strength of their predecessors. Neil Jordan, renowned for his film *The Crying Game,* admits that he took up screenwriting as a way to escape the influence of Joyce. But these literary ancestors have bequeathed a significant gift: their stubborn refusal to yield to the governing forces of their day helped pave the way for their successors. Most of them fled Ireland at one stage, bitter at the stultifying strictures of the Catholic church, disenchanted by lack of support. Beckett declared he'd rather live in France during the war than Ireland in peacetime. Joyce's *Ulysses* was a taboo word in Dublin for many years, and sold on the quiet, hidden inside a brown paper bag, hush, hush, like contraband. There was a dark joke circulating in the early sixties: if you were banned, you knew you'd made it.

You might say, then, that John McGahern "made it" with his grim, 1966 novel *The Dark,* which brazenly addresses incest and abuse, and was seized by Irish custom officials when it arrived from London. The book, a grueling, heartbreaking read, set a new standard for Irish writers, but it cost McGahern his job as a schoolteacher.

Then 1968 came, and with it a fresh wind. The censorship board eased up on its stentorian dictates. And free secondary education was introduced, which eventually would produce an informed citizenry, less willing to board the emigrant ship or plane.

Of course, gainful employment is an elusive quantity in Ireland, and even today it hemorrhages out its young, qualified people to other, more welcoming ports. And even if many of the expatriates return home regularly, making them more commuters than emigrants, it is testament to the continuing flow that this year's Frankfurt Book Fair has chosen as its theme *The Irish Diaspora.* After father-son relationships, religion, land, and politics, emigration is a favorite theme of Irish writers. James Ryan's first novel, *Home from England,* captures the wavering fidelities of the reluctant emigrant, who inhabits neither the old nor the new world, but rather flails in some purgatorial netherworld of memory.

Still, the literary *hejira* may have peaked. The last decade has seen the emergence of myriad young, native writers, the flowering of many publishing houses, and a growing confidence in the native sod. Forty years ago, fewer than two hundred books were published in the entire country.

That wizened, old, married couple, church and state, experiencing marital struggles of its own, is feeling the strain of these changes. Several mouth-numbing scandals within the Catholic church have caused a gradual erosion of trust among its faithful. Last fall's divorce referendum epitomized the growing rift in this country, when the votes for and against were split almost down the middle. After a recount, the pro-divorce side won, by a sliver. By the tiniest margin, a formerly inconceivable change has taken place in this fading outpost of the Vatican, or, as John Ardagh wryly puts it, the "Pope's last hope." And even though the church is contesting the outcome, the fact that it passed at all is an indication that Ireland is ready for change, that the old, traditional ways are no longer working. You can tell the church is losing its grip when the first two books you find on the display rack of a bookshop, are entitled respectively, *Strong Pagans* and *The Atheist*.

As the capital city, Dublin is perhaps the site of the most noticeable developments. Its changing face is hard to describe. When I was a child, my father took us to the top of Dublin's tallest building as a birthday treat. Liberty Hall, overlooking the notorious river Liffey, was about eleven stories tall. Today, an injection of foreign investment has sent skyscrapers and housing developments mushrooming. The inner-city row houses sung of mournfully in the old ballads have virtually disappeared, and in their stead, a sprawl of project housing darts like arteries out to the suburbs.

This growth has given rise to a new generation of urban writers, such as Dermot Bolger, Joseph O'Connor, and Roddy Doyle, whose swaggering, urban realism depicts Dublin not as a charming metropolis, a cultural mecca, but as a black hole full of misbegotten vagrants. Their characters are more likely to hail from the inner city and to speak in Dublin dialect than to be Trinity college graduates. The girls aren't worrying about grades or careers; they're wondering how their new boy-friend—a skinny, teenage kid with pimples and a mohawk, say—will react to the news of his impending fatherhood. These stories are gritty portraits of contemporary city life, about people trying to triumph over their lot in life, to sing their way out of the troubles, as in Roddy Doyle's novel-turned-movie, *The Commitments.*

To illustrate the shift in climate, consider the National Leaving Certificate Curriculum in my high-school years (early seventies). I read Peig Sayer's autobiography of her life on the Blasket Islands, when the potential loss of local fisherman to the wild seas was the overriding worry. A gentle tale of a life that's dying out, it was tame, even bland. Today, two decades on, the Irish Education Board is seriously considering Roddy Doyle's *Paddy Clarke Ha Ha Ha* for inclusion on the curriculum. This is a tale of a city kid's coming of age, rendered in Doyle's inimitable Dublin street argot, that would have been considered blasphemous once. Remember that until recently, Molly Bloom's self-arousal soliloquy on the beach was deemed scandalous. Today, Doyle is touted as the new Joyce, not just a popular hero, but a literary one, having recently won England's esteemed Booker Prize.

Doyle has tried his hand at screen- and playwriting, to varying effects. His television series, *Family,* caused an outcry and fueled a national debate. Like Synge or Joyce, who held the mirror up to the natives, Doyle found himself accused of scurrilous misrepresentation of his subjects. No one wanted to believe that urban family life could be so bleak. Yet people can't resist Doyle's unerring feel for the theatrical, even if it strikes a tender nerve. He is the sort of writer, as Joe O'Connor points out, that people should "have a position on." Doyle is now working on a novel about the wife in the television series, who finds release from her miserable life in large quantities of alcohol. Its tentative title is *The Woman Who Walked into Doors.*

Joe O'Connor, a novelist and journalist who spent many years in London, writes with a witty, often acerbic tone. He's a sort of self-anointed arbiter of contemporary style and culture, all the better positioned being the brother of that once-bald, equally-vociferous singer, Sinéad. You'll find articles by him about political prisoners in serious newspapers, or his assessment of the vigorous Dublin social scene in the European *Cosmopolitan,* for example. His collected essays, assembled under the titillating title *The Secret World of the Irish Male,* was a huge seller last year. While not divulging all of the esoteric habits of that ineffable subspecies, he does write with a heartening honesty of the father-son relationship, an uneasy one historically in this country, where the male is encouraged to be macho, tough, and absolutely never, ever to show himself capable of emotion until he is sufficiently tanked. One of the subheadings of an essay is "Irishmen and Alcohol: A Love Story." You get the picture!

Dermot Bolger, a versatile and tireless writer, whose play recently had a successful run at Dublin's historic Abbey theatre, writes of urban life with a verbal alacrity and a dark undertone that Joyce'd be proud of. He also writes a weekly newspaper column about TV, and has compiled the reputable *Picador Book of Contemporary Irish Fiction* (which sports an upmarket cover of Marilyn Monroe, no joke, reading *Ulysses,* no less).

It is not only the cityscape that comes under the scrutiny of Irish writers: like John McGahern, both Patrick McCabe and Colum McCann write harrowing tales of life in the provinces. McCabe's *Butcher Boy* is a *tour-de-force* tale of a young boy's gradual descent into madness, courageously recounted in the first person. It is a stream-of-consciousness nightmare, a journey through the murky, brutal landscape of Francie Brady's mind. Colum McCann explores this terrain as well, but he also charts newer territories, like San Francisco and Mexico. And he is not afraid to write from a female perspective either, or to incorporate a primal magical realism into his work.

Michael Collins, the grandson of the Irish Nationalist hero, lends another strong voice to the numbers. His fictional milieu is often tough, violent, and focuses on the north of Ireland. A particularly eerie story concerns an IRA hit man who flees to

New York, where he receives an unusual welcome from the Irish Underground. Still finding his voice, Collins has already a remarkable facility for creating atmosphere. He can set a scene that alternately draws you in and repels you. He's not the sort of writer you'd want to pick up right before a meal, though.

In recent years, it has been heartening to witness the emergence of more female writers. In the past, Irish women tended to fulfill their domestic, familial obligations first, putting off till their autumn years what might have been regarded then as creative indulgence. However, now you'll find books published by writers still in their teens. The poet Sara Berekley was a virtual child prodigy. Emma Donoghue is another young novelist who has received notice for her literary promise. Her fiction addresses, candidly and often wittily, the travails of lesbian life in the city. She is helping open doors previously shut to women.

Recently, a group of Irish feminists put together a revisionist collection of fairy tales, wherein the Seven Dwarves, for example, make a strong case for their own union, and Prince Charming is no longer a dashing savior, but rather a wimpish lad with a foot fetish! Then, there are Anne Enright's quirky stories, and Mary Morrissy's extravagant, limber prose. Many of these women, and their male peers, have English publishers and so are known on both sides of the Channel. And several are gaining stature on this side of the Atlantic. Mary Morrissy is a recent recipient of one of America's prestigious Lannan Foundation Awards for Literature.

A discussion of Irish women writers would be incomplete without mention of that *grande dame* of Irish scribblers, Edna O'Brien, whose lusty, sensuous accounts of Irish country life guaranteed her absence on Irish bookshelves for years. Obsessed with the vagaries of love, she has been dubbed by one critic as "the leading cardiologist of broken hearts." She, however, has taken up residence in England, as has her compatriot and exceptionally insightful writer, William Trevor, both of whom have declared at various times that, while they miss their home country, they need distance in order to achieve perspective.

Several years ago, the mostly-male literary powers-that-be convened and decided to compile the definitive anthology of Irish literature, a comprehensive collection of the country's best writing, in English and Irish, from day one to the present. What emerged was a hefty, three-volume compendium, *Field Day.* You'd think that would be the last word on Irish writing, but heavens, no, it was only the beginning. People regarded the anthology as "old whines in new bottles." And the women's community came out *en masse,* excoriating against the marginal inclusion of their gender. They caused such a stir that a fourth volume is in the works, to include literature composed solely by women.

There has always been a mostly healthy debate between the sexes in Ireland, in a country where schools are segregated, leaving boys and girls to grow up regarding the opposite sex as strangers, sometimes as the enemy. Roddy Doyle captures humorously the resultant awkwardness in his fictional milieu. But in the real world, the dialogue and contention continues. The internationally-renowned poet, Eavan Boland, a sophisticated, elegant lyricist, and an articulate spokesperson for her sex, prays in one poem, weary of being relegated to the role of woman as muse: "Help us to escape youth and beauty." Enough, she says, of that "hostile male hegemony." Such blatant articulations have led her to be labeled in one review as "belligerently feminine."

Boland is not alone. The mystical Belfast poet Medbh McGuckian resists being referred to as "a wallpaper poet, writing about begonias." And Nuala Ní Dhomhnaill has said that women "are not taken seriously. We are still put away in the women's quarters, veiled and hidden, and not given full spiritual and mental citizenship." But she turns the stereotype on its head, speaking of Nobel Laureate Seamus Heaney in an interview: "Sometimes I think that his great strength is that he is actually a woman—a great, big, benevolent mountain, standing protectively behind you, like your mother should do."

Divided choices between emigration and staying put, between male and female, between old and new, city and country, are not the only ones running like fracture lines through the Irish landscape. Language is another issue fraught with conflicting opinions. The native tongue, Irish or Gaelic, is now mostly spoken in rural outposts, or "gaeltacht" areas. The time is long gone since Maire Mhac an tSaoi grew up thinking *Treasure Island* was an Irish novel, "because my uncle read it to us in Irish, translating by sight from the English as he went along." Although the government has made huge efforts to resurrect it, some feel it is a moribund tongue, going the way of Latin or Greek—especially those who want to shed their isolationist, insular past and merge with the modern world. This sentiment is at odds with the traditionalists, who have been fighting vigorously to keep Irish "on the cultural menu." Kerry-born Nuala Ní Dhomhnaill vehemently refuses to say die. In a recent *New York Times* article, she referred to Gaelic as "the corpse who sat up and talked back." And while Ní Dhomhnaill lives, the corpse will keep flexing its brittle bones. "One thing that makes me get up in the morning," she says, "is the desire to take Irish back from that grey-faced, Irish-revivalist, male preserve. I'll be damned if I'll let them monopolise the language."

Biddy Jenkinson, in agreement, forbids her work to be translated into English, which she describes as "a small, rude gesture to those who think that everything can be harvested and stored without loss in an English-speaking Ireland."

Michael Hartnett is another pioneer of Irish, who in a courageous bid to espouse his native language wholly, declared in 1975, on the publication of his book *A Farewell to*

English, that he would henceforth write only in Irish. Sadly, barely a decade later, Hartnett had to recant, for it's hard enough to earn a wage as a writer, let alone as a writer of a language only a few people read.

Yet, according to Bord na Leabhar Gaeilge, the Irish Language Books Board, the future looks promising, Irish books today taking up twelve to sixteen percent of the market. In a recent *Books Ireland* article, Séan de Freine, the board's director, claims that Irish is "no longer a linguistic relic," and points to the proliferation of schools which teach through Irish. But with only a handful of adults capable of waxing lyrical for you *as gaeilge,* it has a long way to go.

The perfect consolation prize for this divided nation might be the recent rapprochement in Northern Ireland, suggesting the possibility of peace for the first time in years, even if relations are still uneasy. Ever since the Troubles erupted again in the mid-sixties, writers have struggled with how to address the conflict in their work. They were accused of opportunism if they wrote about it, evasion if they didn't. Seamus Heaney, who avoided the north as subject matter for years, felt the dilemma to be a paucity of appropriate symbols. Seamus Deane wryly pointed out that artists "can often be more troubled by the *idea* that they should be troubled—by the Troubles—than by the idea itself." Some theatres adopted "a culture of aloofness" for fear of jeopardizing funding. Ciarán Carson has been one of the more vocal writers on the situation in his native Belfast, which he refers to as the "world capital of knee surgeons," an ironic testament to the high incidence of kneecapping by terrorists.

Then there are those who vehemently resist affiliation with their native turf. Writers set their imaginary compasses toward England or America or Mexico. John Banville looks to Europe for his subject matter. A writer of lean, poetic prose, he takes on historical figures such as Copernicus, say, or Kepler, and situates them in a fictional milieu, which he conjures with a rigorous exactitude. Not for the restless reader, his books are dense and cerebral, laden with closely observed detail. In an interview, he has said, "The artist's only responsibility is to create masterpieces, he has no duty to society. I want to get away from 'Irish' themes or from having to comment on Ireland today."

And Banville may have his reasons: Ireland is like a small town. I've never run into an Irish person abroad who doesn't ask, "Ye wouldn't happen to know so-and-so, would ye?" And nine times out of ten, I'll know someone who knows someone who knows so-and-so's sister. Such close-knit connections can lead to problems. One Dublin writer bemoans his fate as a literary critic, which task—to evaluate work candidly—is compounded by the knowledge that he might run into the subject of his review on his way to the mailbox.

And lord knows, it's a hard place to write in. Such social pressures to yield to: literary workshops, festivals, readings. A week doesn't go by but one county or another is having its grand annual gala of literary activity. And then there are the heavyweights, which cannot be missed—Listowel Writers Week, Galway Arts Fest, Dublin Theatre Festival. There must be an event per capita per month. How is a person to sit home and scribble in his or her cold kitchen when such social responsibility calls?

But, heaven help us, lest you think everyone in this place is a book buff, let it be known that there are other allegiances of even greater import: This, a headline from a provincial newspaper last summer: "Salmon Rushdie Spotted in Sligo." Whether anyone netted him or not remains a mystery.

The complex fissures lineating the Irish landscape seem to be almost an historical birthright, like rain or stout. While some people laud the onslaught of new writers, the virtual renaissance, others, like Thomas Kinsella, wonder aloud just how many will endure. And Denis Driscoll is far from convinced that all the hullaballoo is a good thing. He wrote recently that "contemporary Irish poetry is in a bad state. Most of it—particularly in the South—is self-indulgent, lifeless, lazy, turgid, sentimental and unimaginative."

There you have it. Choose your side. Maybe Joe O'Connor puts it best when he says, "The great thing about being an Irish writer is that there's always something to write against. There's always a windmill to tilt at." Or a fierce wind to wag your impassioned pen into.

Suggested Reading List

Fiction
John Banville: *Mefisto, The Book of Evidence*
Dermot Bolger: *The Journey Home*
Michael Collins: *The Man Who Dreamt of Lobsters*
Evelyn Conlon: *My Head Is Opening*
Roddy Doyle: *The Commitments, The Snapper, The Van, Paddy Clarke Ha Ha Ha*
Anne Enright: *The Portable Virgin*
Emma Donoghue: *Stir Fry, Hood*
Nena Fitzgerald: *Fables of the Irish Intelligensia*
Dermot Healy: *A Goat's Song*
Neil Jordan: *Sunrise with Sea Monster*
Benedict Kiely: *Proxopera, Nothing Happens in Carmincross*
Sean MacMathuna: *The Atheist*
Patrick McCabe: *The Butcher Boy, The Dead School*
Colum McCann: *Fishing the Sloe-Black River, Songdogs*
John McGahern: *The Dark, Amongst Women, Leavetaking*
Mary Morrissy: *Mother of Pearl*
Christopher Nolan: *Under the Eye of the Clock*
Edna O'Brien: *A Fanatic Heart*
Joseph O'Connor: *Cowboys and Indians, Desperadoes, True Believers, The Secret World of the Irish Male*
James Ryan: *Home from England*

Writing out of Ireland: A Terrible Beauty Is Reborn

Colm Toibín: *The Heather Blazing, The Sign of the Cross*
William Trevor: Everything!

Poets
Eavan Boland, Paul Durcan, Eamon Grennan, Michael Hartnett, Brendan Kennelly, Paula Meehan, Nuala Ní Dhomhnaill
Northern Poets:
Medbh McGuckian, Seamus Heaney, Ciarán Carson, Derek Mahon, Michael Longley

Collections
The Picador Book of Contemporary Irish Fiction,
   Ed. Dermot Bolger
A Rage for Order: Poetry of the Northern Ireland Troubles,
   Ed. Frank Ormsby
Field Day, Four-volume anthology of Irish Literature

Excerpts:

People regard my books as Gothic extravaganzas, but I see them as realism; one has only to go down the street to see how full of Gothic extravagance life is. I think of my novels as sonnet sequences, and I may spend up to a year writing the first paragraph.

—John Banville

The Death of Irish
The tide gone out for good
31 words for seaweed
whiten on the foreshore
        —Aidan Matthews

Annie Callan

Ireland
A Volkswagen parked in the gap,
But gently ticking over.
You wonder if it's lovers,
and not men hurrying back across
two fields and a river.
                              —Paul Muldoon

V: The Northern Ireland Question
two wee girls
were playing tag near a car…

how many counties would you say
are worth their scattered fingers?
                              —Padraic Fiacc

The Men in My Life
And when night comes we will feel no need
To deceive our wives. Under pink black skies
And a solitary oak tree I will be at home
With my woman. He will be at home with his wife.
We are gay brothers and in a free Ireland
Brotherly gaiety is one of the forms of marriage.
                              —Paul Durcan

*Eddie Virago, twenty-four, sporting a mohawk, heading to London in
search of work. On the boat across, he meets a girl:*
    On the train [to London], they got off with each other and
Eddie was glad he'd dropped into the men's room of Holyhead
Station to brush his teeth and get his act together with one of
those pathetic traveller kits you buy for two quid fifty and then

76   *Glimmer Train Stories*

immediately regret. She kissed him hard. Their teeth scraped. Her lips were cold. She smelt of anise and soap. The way she kissed him, she sort of ground her lips against him, as though they were dunking for apples in a basinful of water at Hallowe'en.

—Joseph O'Connor, *Cowboys and Indians*

The worst was to have to sleep with him the nights he wanted love, strain of waiting for him to come to bed, no hope of sleep in the waiting—counting and losing the count of the thirty-two boards across the ceiling, trying to pick out the darker circles of the knots beneath the varnish. Watch the moon on the broken brass bells at the foot of the bed. Turn and listen and turn. Go over the day that was gone, what was done or left undone, or dream of the dead days with her in June.

The dreams and passing of time would break with the noise of the hall door opening, feet on the cement, his habitual noises as he drank barley water over the dying fire, and at last the stockinged feet on the stairs.

He was coming and there was nothing to do but wait and grow hard as stone and lie.

"Are you sleeping?"

The one thing was to keep the eyes shut no matter what and to lie stiff as a board.

"You're asleep so?"

It was such breathing relief to hear the soft plump of his clothes being let fall on the floor. And then the winding of the clock.

A sudden pause instead of him pulling back the sheets, he was fumbling through the heap of clothes on the floor. A match struck and flared in the dark. It was brought close. He could feel the heat on his face. His lids lit up like blood-soaked curtains. With a cry he turned sideways and brought his hands to his face. When he could look, the flame had burned down the black char of matchwood to Mahoney's fingers, and his face was ugly with suspicion.

"You were quick to wake?"

He'd have to pull himself together to answer.

"I was sleeping. I felt something."

The match flame had burned out.

"You didn't seem to be sleeping much to me?"

"I was sleeping. I got frightened."

Hatred took the place of fear, and it brought the mastery of not caring much more. No one had right to bring a match burning close to his face in the night to see if he was sleeping or not.

—John McGahern, *The Dark*

Maria (rhymes with Pariah) has just revealed to her friend that her roommates are gay:

"They're perfectly normal people otherwise," Maria looked up suspiciously. "And you're not to spread it round campus."

"I wouldn't." Yvonne's voice was hurt. "I can just imagine how I'd feel if a rumor went round college about me—I'd be sure everyone was staring. I won't even tell Pete, I promise."

"Thanks."

Yvonne sat back, dazed. "I just hope no one jumps to the wrong conclusions about you, Maria."

"Sorry?"

Yvonne had got her breath back. "Just because you live with them, I mean. Not that anyone would be likely to, since you've got hair down to your shoulders and you often wear skirts. Well, fairly often."

Maria rested her forehead on the heel of her hand. "Look, they're both very nice. And they wear skirts sometimes too."

"Oh, I know," said Yvonne, wisely, "but they'd have to, wouldn't they, as cover?"

—Emma Donoghue, *Stir Fry*

Writing out of Ireland: A Terrible Beauty Is Reborn

Francie Brady interviews for a job at the butcher's shop:

You'll have to be up and out at the crack of dawn he says, what do you think of that? I said that's fine Mr Leddy. Any man thinks this work is easy needs his head examined—you want to be tough to work here! Indeed you do Mr Leddy I said and I could see he liked me calling him that so I kept on doing it. It wouldn't have been a good idea to say I suppose you should know all these things considering you are a pig yourself with your big pig head but I would have liked to say it the way he was going on. Like he was some kind of visiting professor down from the Cutting Up Pigs University. The more he talked the more he wanted to talk. Pigs, by Mr Leddy. That was what I thought, but I kept on nodding away. O yes. And, Hmmm. If you don't pull your weight he says its down that road straight away. I've no time for wasters. O you'll have no trouble with me Mr Leddy I says. Good he says for I daresay they're not falling over themselves giving you jobs about this town.

—Patrick McCabe, *The Butcher Boy*

—Jesus, I wouldn't like tha', said Yvonne. —Some dirty oul' bastard with a rubber glove.

—It was a woman, said Sharon.

—Yeah?

—Yeah. She was very nice. Doctor Murray. She was real young as well. It took bleedin' ages though.

—How long, abou'? Mary asked her.

—Ages. Hours. Most of it was waitin' though. All fuckin' mornin', I'm not jokin' yeh. She said it was because of the cut-backs. She kept sayin' it. She said I should write to me TD (representative).

—The stupid bitch, said Jackie.

They laughed.

—Ah, she was nice, said Sharon. —Come here though. I nearly died, listen. She said she wanted to know me menstrual history an' I didn't know what she was talkin' abou' till she told me. I felt like a right f—in' eejit. I knew what it meant, like, but I was—

    —Why didn't she just say your periods? said Yvonne.

    —Doctors are always like tha', said Sharon.

    —Menstrual history, said Jackie. —I got a *C* in that in me Inter. They roared.

—Roddy Doyle, The Snapper

The girls playing hopscotch among the peelings or swinging languidly from a lamppost barely looked up as she wandered, like a careful ghost, through the battered landscape of their games. It was the season for skipping. Thwack of rope and a strange, sour chanting. Or they stood idly in twos and threes chewing the split ends of their hair as Irene threaded her way through them intent only on their own whispered secrets. There were small boys crouched in knots over games of marbles, their mittens sewn with elastic to their hand-me-down coats. They seemed in thrall to the glassy baubles shot through with seams of ocher and Prussian blue and would have registered Irene only as another pair of mottled female legs passing by.

—Mary Morrissy, Mother of Pearl

Each man in the hospital sets up house for the night, and breaks camp the following morning. Next begins the arduous task of walking.

Walking, along the same path if necessary, walking with eyes down and intent, walking without sympathy, walking in the scent of another creature with the head arrogantly back, stalking feverishly, stopping to listen, stopping as if there was another following you as you followed someone who wasn't there, walking, sometimes in slippers but mostly going back to the boots you wore the first day you came into the hospital...

In their boots the Mayo men walk to the end of the corridor, turn and tramp back; neighbouring men, fags burning next the little finger, butterflies in their stomachs, dogs at their heels, and animals looking over hedges at them. When you've found someone to walk with you're happy, even when that someone is yourself.

—Dermot Healy, *A Goat's Song*

My older sister, Brigid, succeeded with a spectacular anorexia. After classes she would sidle off into the bog, to a large rock where nobody could see her, her school sandwiches in her pocket, her Bible in her hand. There she would perch like a raked robin, and bit by bit she would tear up the bread, like a sacrament, and throw it all around her. The rock had a history— in penal times it had been used as a meeting place for mass. I sometimes watched her from a distance. She was a house of bones, my sister, throwing her bread away. Once, out on the rock, I saw her take my father's pliers to her fingers and slowly pluck out the nail from the middle finger of her left hand. She did it because she had heard that it was what the Cromwellians had done to the harpists in the seventeenth century, so they could no longer pluck the catgut to make music. She wanted to know how it felt. Her finger bled for days. She told our father that she had caught her hand in a school door.

—Colum McCann, "Sisters"

The play did not pass off without incident. The teacher's cousin Milo was drunk, belligerent, and offensive. He called girls up to the fire to pretend to talk to them and then touched the calves of their legs and tickled the backs of their knees. He called me up and asked would I click. He was an auctioneer from the city and unmarried. The teacher's two sons also came to look at the performance, but one of them left in the middle. He was strange and would laugh for no reason, and although over twenty he called the teacher "Mammy." He had very bright-red hair and a peculiar stare in his eyes. For the most part, the infants forgot their lines, lost their heads, and the prompter was always late, so that the wrong girls picked up her cues. She was behind a curtain but could be heard out on the street. The whole thing was a fiasco.

—Edna O'Brien, *The Doll*

Afterlives
The orators yap, and guns
Go off in a back street;
But the faith does not die

That in our time these things
Will amaze the literate children
In their non-sectarian schools
And the dark places be
Ablaze with love and poetry
When the power of good prevails.

—Derek Mahon

ANNIE CALLAN now lives in Portland, Oregon, where she serves as consulting editor for *Glimmer Train.* Her collection of poems, *The Back Door,* was published last fall by Trask House Press. She is currently working on a series of personal essays about Ireland.

Excerpt from

What Is She Like?

A PERSONALITY BOOK FOR GIRLS

By

MARY BROCKMAN

1936

Illustrations by George Wright

RELATIONS WITH PEOPLE

Boys admire good looks and you should make the most of your own. Remember that the foundation is particular personal cleanliness and that, first of all, boys like girls who are beautifully clean.

Boys like cheerful girls. They will expect you to keep your good humor, and will tell you to "snap out" of a mood. They run, when they can, from feminine fits of temperament.

Boys don't want girls to talk too much or try to appear too wise. While they like a certain amount of assurance, they want girls to know when to sit back and look interested. The best "line" with any young man is to make him feel important.

Boys like girls who can join in things. If you want them to find you good company, learn to dance well and to swim and skate and play a good game of bridge. See to your education in baseball, football, and whatever fills the sports page of the day. Entertain boys in your home no matter how modest it is, and give them something good to eat.

Abigail Thomas

*This is a photo of me in a wicker carriage in back of my
grandmother's big old house in Flushing, New York. I guess it was
about 1943. My grandma used to bang on the pipes in the kitchen
to waken the children sleeping on the third floor, very effective.
Everything smelled like bacon. There were wonderful hydrangeas out
front, and in the back you could peek over a wall and see the Long
Island Railroad trains going back and forth, which was exciting. I
still dream about that backyard which is now an apartment house.*

Abigail Thomas's collection of stories, *Getting Over Tom,* and her first novel,
An Actual Life, have recently been published. She has also published three
books for children.

Thomas lives in New York City, and enjoys the time she spends writing and
running a writing workshop.

ABIGAIL THOMAS
Herb's Pajamas

Rudy Cervantes died on my back stairs and although I'm sorry for his death I couldn't have saved him. Not even if I'd denied him the little bit of pleasure we'd both grown used to. Still, it's the worst that's happened so far. Rudy was a good soul but he smoked. I tried that once, choked, and let my body tell me something, but Rudy liked his cigarette after the act of love and since I forbade smoking in the bedroom, he'd generally light up in the hall then go down the back stairs and sit in the kitchen. This made him feel peaceful enough to go home. One time he said he wished he could stay all the way through to breakfast and after. But we knew that wasn't in the cards. We never wanted to worry May. We never meant for her to have to let on that she knew, if she did know. If she woke up and missed him sometimes, she never said so.

But he died. It was such a surprise. We had had a fine time as always, and he'd said he was coming back upstairs for another half hour after he had his Winston. I waited and fell asleep, draping the sheet over my thigh the way that made me look most delicious due to the path the moon takes on my bed, and when I woke it was three-thirty. I turned to look at the clock, and no Rudy. It wasn't like him not to say good-bye and besides there were his trousers neatly folded on the back of the chair, and in that moment I knew something had happened to the sweetest of men. I put on my bathrobe and slippers and I even combed my hair, knowing what I would find, and I wanted to be dressed respectfully because there was no other reason for Rudy not to be either in my bed or his own except that death had claimed him. And there he was, sitting on the landing in the back stairs, the cigarette still in his fingers holding a tremendously long ash.

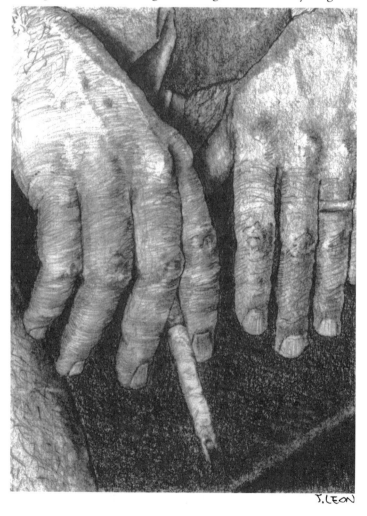

J.LEON

He must have died instantly and slid down the wall like an ice cream melting. He looked so natural there. But he didn't look lifelike; I knew he was dead. The real Rudy would have looked up from being aware of my perfume, but he didn't stir. Then I began to think he had meant to sit there. Maybe he hadn't gone down to the kitchen, or had gone down and come partway back. Maybe he had seen a mouse or something. Rudy did hate the sight of a mouse. It made the tears spring to my eyes to see him like that, my heart nearly stopped on its own. "Oh Rudy," I whispered, "already I am missing you," and as if in answer I heard the wind start to kick up outside. Poor Rudy—I felt of him then, and his hands and face were cold but he wasn't stiff yet anywhere if you get my drift; really I just wanted to say good-bye to every part of him. Rudy would have understood that, I think. He was wearing Herbert's pajama top, which I always made him do. "Do you want to catch your death of cold?" I would say to him. So he would compromise with the top half. It didn't catch fire from his cigarette either; Herbert was a nut for inflammable. So poor Rudy died of a heart attack pure and simple and although I am sorry, if it was to be I am glad enough it happened here after a night of love instead of next door while May snored away and he stared at the patterns of leaves on the ceiling.

Still, it was an inconvenience. I never made a secret of my life, but neither did I broadcast it, and we had never meant to harm May in any way, or rub her nose in it, as it were. But the truth is that May had not cared for the act of love for many years now; her favorite was a box of jelly doughnuts and a pack of Tareytons where as I, as they say, could not seem to tire of it. Even at my age, which was sixty. Rudy had thrown a pebble at my window once and that was the start of it. Rudy used to say to me, "You know what I like about you, Belle?" "What, Rudy?" I'd answer. "You're old, like me," he'd say, and we'd both laugh, although these lines were not original with Rudy;

I had read them somewhere myself between the pages of a magazine. But you can't put a padlock on humor. And I took no offense, either, because while I'm old I know a few things, and my form is just as nice as ever it was, never having been weighed down by childbearing and always being supported by the best foundation garments money can buy. May is younger but as I said not much interested in things of the flesh to do with Rudy. Anyway, here was my dilemma: there was a dead husband on my back stairs and he wasn't mine. I had to get him out of there and back to his own front porch. This presented a problem since I am barely five feet four and Rudy himself was not a big man but there is some truth in the term *dead weight*. Rudy alive I think I could have carried across the room and up the stairs if he had asked me to, but Rudy dead was another matter. There was no breath in him. The fact is I could not move Rudy one inch myself. On top of that I knew that bodies began to freeze in their positions and I wasn't sure how much time I had.

There was no one for me to turn to but Edna, and I didn't want to scare her with a ringing phone at this hour of the night, seeing as how her house is so big around her; but dawn was fast approaching and Rudy needed to be on his own porch swing in less than an hour. When she picked up the phone I didn't tell her exactly what was wrong, but I said, "Edna, it's me, Belle. I need you to come here on the double-quick. It's a matter of life and death. No time for questions. Don't make a sound." Edna has such good heart that she was here in no time, with her hair in those pink, rubber curlers and wearing her huge, pink night-gown with the tiny roses on it. Edna is a big woman. I was waiting at the back door and said right off, "Sit down, Edna. Rudy's dead on my back stairs. He died here tonight smoking a cigarette." Edna crossed herself. She sat down.

"What?" she said.

"You heard me. It's true. And we've got to get him out of here before the whole world wakes up," I said, pointing

meaningfully at the window out of which you could see the dark
shape that was Rudy and May's ugly house. But Edna just sat
there. Edna has been my best friend since we were born, but May
is her second best, so you can see how Edna might be torn in her
loyalties until she thought about it. I pointed out that May would
hate to find that her husband had died in another woman's
house. Edna never approved of the way I took up with Rudy,
as she puts it. "When was I ever asking for approval?" I asked.
Of course she knew she had no answer to that. "Come with
me," I said. "We have to get him out of here."

At first Edna was nervous as a kitten since she had never set
eyes on a naked man, but then I had never seen a dead one. But
I reminded her Rudy wasn't naked. He was wearing Herb's
pajamas. So we climbed the stairs holding hands and we looked
at the poor man together. I didn't feel like saying anything. He
looked different already in the five minutes I'd been gone.
Different how, I can't explain. Edna crossed herself again.
"Glory be," she said, which sounded old-fashioned, but Edna is
old-fashioned. Her favorite movie star is Fred Astaire. Then
Edna said, "He isn't dressed, Belle."

I said, "Well, not in his street clothes, Edna."

"Does he have anything on under that shirt?" she asked, and
I had to say I wasn't sure. I wasn't; I couldn't remember. "Well,
I can't touch him then. Belle, you know I never have even seen
that thing," and she wouldn't go near him until I'd assured her
that he was wearing his underpants. I prayed the Lord that he
was, and I was right. Poor Rudy. He wore little red-checked
boxer shorts that May bought for him by the dozen from her
sister-in-law who got them cheap. But he never minded. Rudy
was a saint among men. All the while I was moaning, which was
not like me at all, and wiping away the tears. Edna said, "Oh,
Belle, I can't touch him. He's dead."

And I said, "Well, I know he's dead, Edna. That's why I called
you here."

"We have to call the police," she said, starting to tremble.

"What is May going to say when she wakes up and can't find her Rudy, and it turns out he's here on my stairs, and I'm your oldest friend in all the world? Do you think you'll be on the chrysanthemum committee?" Well, I hated to hurt her where she lived, but I had no choice. We were running out of time.

"Maybe if I get under his arms," she said, and somehow she did with a scooping motion and we got him over her shoulder. By now he was stiffening up a little, and it was awkward to get him down the stairs; but the weight was no problem for Edna who is as I said six feet nothing and one hundred sixty pounds. She cried the whole way, in tiny little mews. "Sshhh," I kept saying.

"I can't shhh," she said. "I am carrying a dead person. I am carrying a dead man. Mew, mew." I wanted to point out it wasn't just any dead man, it was Rudy Cervantes, who had repaired our shoes for thirty years, but I was feeling too bad myself to bring it up.

And Edna managed beautifully. Down the back stairs, across the linoleum, out my screen door which I held open praying the dogs wouldn't start barking, down the porch steps (three), onto and across the path. Edna is strong. She chops her own wood. She makes her own bread. She hauls her own water. And she carried poor Rudy Cervantes all the way across my yard and his, and up his porch steps, and placed him on his own porch swing which I held steady for her. Then the trouble was he was still wearing Herb's pajamas. I couldn't think of anything to do but take them off. That left Rudy in his underpants on the porch swing, but I threw a blanket over him that they kept on the rocker and I gave him a kiss on the top of his cold head. Edna said, "I hope I don't burn in hell for my part in this." And she went home. And so did I. Thank God all the dogs in the neighborhood were miraculously asleep throughout this. But I have given love freely and sometimes God cuts me a little slack.

THOM JONES
Short-story writer and novelist-in-training

Interview
by Jim Schumock

Short-story writer extraordinaire and novelist-in-training, Thom Jones was born in Aurora, Illinois, in 1945. He is the author of two collections of short stories: The Pugilist at Rest, *and most recently* Cold Snap, *just published by Little, Brown.*

Thom Jones

SCHUMOCK: *I've been told that an interview you saw with fellow Iowa Writers Workshop attendee Tracy Kidder stimulated you to begin publishing your work. Is that true?*

JONES: Well, yes, most of my life I think I was wasting time— running marathons, swimming, boxing, lifting weights, and I remember I was working as a janitor. I had just won a trip around the world by writing a little ad jingle—I had been an ad writer, and I got back and I remember we were in a transition house—

it was really sort of a dump—waiting to buy a house. And I came home from the graveyard shift and cracked a six-pack of Rainier's Ale, and I remember drinking a few. I was sitting there in my janitor's shirt, which was sort of like a bowling shirt (it shone in the dark), and there was Tracy, an old friend from Iowa, talking to Tom Brokaw. And I thought, *Ooh, what have I been doing? I have sort of let my life get out of control here. I'd like to write again.* But I didn't at that time; I got drunk instead and continued to work and just think about it, and finally when I bought a computer, just after my daughter was born, I started writing. And almost immediately I published.

What was your time like when you were at the Iowa Writers Workshop?

Oh, it was great. Stuart Dybek was there—there were a lot of very good writers there. Denis Johnson was there. Ray Carver was there. John Cheever. Frederick Exley, Jon Jackson, Richard Yates. Wonderful writers.

So you really had a very long apprenticeship before you hit the scene, didn't you?

Yes. My whole plan had been to be an ad writer. When I graduated from the University of Washington I had a job lined up. I had been parking cars and this guy used to come over with an Austin-Healey, and I asked, "How did you get that?" He said, "Well, you know, the ad agency gives us a car." And I thought, *I'm pretty good at that.* My mother was an ad writer. And he said, "Well, show us what you got." And he liked it, and so I had this job. I couldn't wait to get this Healey, but my professors at Washington said, "Try to get into Stanford and Iowa—nobody from Washington's ever gotten in and you have a good chance." So I did it, and they both accepted me, and I heard that Iowa was the best place, so off I went.

Did you really read a book a day for ten years at one point?

That's right. When I was working as a custodian, I would get stacks of library books. Olympia, Washington, has three very good libraries—the state library, a university library, and a Timberland system—so I always had twenty-five books by my bedside, and maybe I'd peruse three or four in a day. If I got something that was really slower reading I would spend a week on it, but all in all, in eleven years I think, roughly speaking, I probably *did* read ten thousand books, and I know that was my real education. Because I wasn't working as a professional, I could think. I was doing mechanical work. I thought about what I would write. I would think about the books I had been reading—I had *time* to think. It's very hard for people who are knocking around in the world to have that kind of leisure.

Who were some of the writers that really stood out at that time for you?

Well, there are so many that it's hard to say. I'm thinking now of Dreiser, Thomas Hardy, Larry Brown, Richard Wright, of Joyce Carol Oates, Celine, Robert Stone, Richard Price, Cormac [McCarthy], Hubert Selby, Jr., Somerset Maugham, Thomas Mann, let me think ... V.S. Naipaul. Kingsley Amis has always been a big one with me—I like the early British Angry Young Men bunch—Alan Sillitoe, John Braine, John Osborne. I'm thinking ... Brian Moore.

I read the Russians a lot—reread the classics—everything, virtually everything. Robert Stone once said, "Being an author is one of the hardest things in the world, because you have to know everything." I mean, you have to know "how things are." You have to know the human heart. A dentist has to know root canals or something, but an author has to know what life is all about.

That's why I think it's hard to become ... most first novelists are about forty years old or whatever. It takes a long time to figure things out and produce. Hemingway wrote *The Sun Also Rises,* I think, when he was twenty-six or twenty-five, and Carson McCullers wrote *The Heart is a Lonely Hunter* when she was twenty-five, but that kind of thing was pretty rare. And, incidentally, Flannnery O'Connor is one of my favorites.

Right—one of my favorites, too. Have you ever read The Habit of Being?

Of course I have. Yes, it's great.

I remember being enchanted and enthralled by Dostoyevsky and all the travails of his life he details in his writer's notebooks: the epileptic seizures, Turgenev avoiding him because he'd borrowed money for gambling. What did Dostoyevsky bring alive in you?

Well, when I was discharged from the Marine Corps, I had a head injury from a boxing match, and I didn't have the classic grand mal syndrome, but rather a variant of temporal-lobe epilepsy with fugue states, which is extremely rare, so I was discharged as a schizophrenic. They didn't quite know what was the matter with me and I can't blame them at all, they were good doctors, but when I got home, my own physician sent me to a Russian neurologist.

And so when I presented myself with these very strange seizures, he handed me a copy of *The Idiot.* He said, "Maybe this will help you figure it out a little bit," and immediately, I embraced Dostoyevsky, read his whole body of work, and absolutely knew that I had to be a writer. I'm in Aurora, working in a factory, that seemed to be my life, until this happened to me, and then I was obsessed with the meaning of life, the existence of God, the riddle of existence, the existential business. I read *Notes from the Underground, The House of the Dead, The Brothers Karamazov, Crime and Punishment,* everything, virtually. I was a madman—tore into all books. I read the great thinkers of the world and wondered, *What do they make of it? What does Plato think?* And also then I found Schopenhauer, and I thought, *How many of these people live by their own proscription?* Very few of them do. Take Buddha, for instance: "... pain is caused by desire— eliminate all earthly desires..." Well, the man had an eating problem. He was immense, if the various statues are any

94

indication. I realized that, basically, it's up to us to just figure our lives out; people are like sheep often, and they want somebody to tell them how to do it, but my whole thing has been individuality and figuring out for yourself. I'm in this bag of skin and it's up to me—I'm responsible for it. I live and die by it, but Dostoyevsky—it was a miracle when I look back, and I see the patterns, how all these things had to happen for me to be here right now.

Swiss writer Robert Walser, one of Kafka's literary fathers, ultimately committed himself to an asylum and didn't write for the last thirty years of his life, saying, "I have not come here to write; I have come here to be mad." Do you ever feel like throwing in the towel and just going mad?

I think that a lot of times a writer will be in a frame of mind… I mean, to have this exquisite perceptual sensitivity, you pay a very big price. And most fiction writers I know have seen the dark night of the soul, so that when you come back from that you may be able to tell your tale, or you may be too shaken to do it. You may be able to hang on and tell your stories for a year or two or three, or for the rest of your life, or you just might go over the edge, into the abyss. I think there are a lot of gifted artists out there who experience this and can never really get it down, because it's happening so fast, and they might be just a shade over the edge—or not a shade, in terms of degrees and velocity of it and the pressure of it. It requires a tremendous amount of discipline to write, and I often feel after I write a story or something, *Boy, there goes six months of my life.* It's hard to do.

You mention Edvard Munch's The Scream *in one of your stories, and I remember the first time I saw it, I went,* Boy, am I glad I don't feel like he does, *but as I've grown older I go,* Gee, I really know how he feels. *Has your sense of that painting evolved over time?*

Of course, and the older you get the more you find out how many nasty little surprises life has in store for you, in terms of health, and I think the wiser you become, the more you see your illusions are erased and the more of a realist you become, and it's not pretty. Sometimes it would be nice, I think, just to be a normal person—optimistic, easygoing, and trusting, and not too obsessed with this business that I'm obsessed with—life and people, the world, and God, and so forth.

The world of many promises and few real offers really exploded for you with the publication of The Pugilist at Rest. *What are the clearest lessons you learned from that experience?*

Well, I learned that the work is the most important thing—that fame, celebrity, money, these things are very hollow. They're very shallow. It was good to be able to do it and see that I could do it. Now I often look back at my days as a janitor as kind of a lost paradise and long for my broom, but I had to do this. I wanted to try it, and I think that with a lot of writers— I learned this as a boxer—the problem oftentimes is that the conscious mind says, *I want to proceed from A to B as the crow flies,* but really they have this subconscious agenda whereby they want to lose. I used to see fighters come in a day before a fight six pounds overweight, and I realized then that they needed to lose or that they needed to have an excuse, because if they got in the best shape of their lives and then lost, they would have to say, "I lost," and not, "I was overweight and I had to make weight." Writers will do that too; instead of going for it, writing from their hearts, giving their best, they will hedge, and then when they're rejected, they say—or when they engage themselves in some sort of ten-year project, you know it's just a way of buying time to avoid the true test—"Can I really do it if I let it go all the way?" And when I decided to go all the way with it, it was *The New Yorker* and the prizes, or nothing. I mean, if my ceiling were going to be the *Seattle Review,* my aspirations ... I couldn't have succeeded had that been the ceiling. I was more grandiose; I believed in myself, and it worked.

I know that you had some offers from Hollywood at that time, too.

I think someone wanted you to write an original screenplay. Was Hollywood just a lot of tinsel for you and not much substance?

Yes, yes, very much so. I mean, I love writing dialogue. Dialogue is my major thing. I remember going down there many times and being given the Hollywood Kiss and so on—with the limousines and meeting stars and whatnot. As I recall, the movie *The Player*—once I saw that, I realized the acquisition and the game and the chase are more important really than the work. As a fiction writer, I am my own God—I can do everything. I have complete and total control of what I'm doing, whereas I think a lot of writers I know who do scripts feel like they're typists, and they have to deal with the egos of producers and people that are *so* wealthy that a writer is just sort of a necessary evil. And I'm really in it for the work—I'm in it to do something good. I want to write something great. I mean, you never seem to do what you set out to do, of course, but you try, and that's what I want to do. I'm not in it for the parties and the goofing around. I work very hard. I work seven days a week, five hours a day, and when I see some students, they'll say, "Do you want to go on a canoe trip with us, Thom?" Or: "Do you want to go backpacking?" I'm thinking, *No, I want to write.* If you want to go backpacking and so on, I don't know if you're going to make it or not, because you've got to deal with obsessed, hard-working people like me. I'm your competition and if you're backpacking, I'm writing, and you're getting weaker and I'm getting stronger.

A number of the stories in The Pugilist at Rest *take place in Vietnam or with people who are going to Vietnam, and I know you didn't really go there. I know you don't claim the background, but do you ever feel guilty writing about the experience?*

I did in the beginning. I thought, *What right do I have to write this?* I had been in the Marine Corps, I'd been in a recon outfit, and when I got my boxing injury, I was discharged. It was a very shameful experience for me, but later the whole company—

except for one fellow—was killed, including my best friend, and ultimately, I married his girl. We've been married twenty-seven years now, Sally and I, and I didn't dare ... You know, I looked at *The Things They Carried* [Tim O'Brien] and I thought, *That's such a perfect story, there's just no way ... who needs to hear what I have to say about Vietnam?* But, as I said, I had been in the Marines, I knew weapons, I knew the tactics, and one day when the Persian Gulf thing was happening, my wife said, "Today's Rolf's birthday," and we both loved him very much, and so I sat down and wrote that story ["The Pugilist at Rest"] for him. It wasn't for me; it was for him, because he was just a wonderful, wonderful guy. So that's how I came to write it.

You're teaching now at the Iowa Writers Workshop, from which you graduated, and I know you avoided academia rather consciously for quite some time. How does it feel from the inside these days?

Well, it's great. You know, Iowa's the first program in the country that had a workshop, and since Frank Conroy's been there he has done a great deal to improve it. Frank loves the workshop. I think if you said anything bad about it, he'd get in a fistfight with you. He's just great. And they have visiting writers come, and I'm one of them. I have followed Denis Johnson. And they asked me to stay another year, and I was happy to do it because I love the students. The quality of their work is very good, and since I am in many of the magazines and know what they want and what they don't want, it's easy for me to line edit. My students are selling books; they're winning prizes; I feel very proud of them ... I love Iowa.

Beyond Vietnam, a lot of your stories have to do with illnesses and doctors. I was wondering ... you seem to be very interested in illnesses. Have you ever met one you didn't like?

Illnesses ... there are so many of them, and I'll sit and read ... I like to read tropical medicine because those are the really great ones. I'm astonished and horrified. It's sort of like reading about a train wreck or something. I have a tremendous imagination, am an incredible hypochondriac, but now that I've lived this long, it's all my fears coming true. I'm really sick, so now I read about diabetes, which I have, and epilepsy, which I have, and depression, which I have, and all these things. I wonder how I go from day to day sometimes.

Are you hypomanic?

When I write, I go into a manic state. When I write in the first voice, I become the character, like a method actor. And I get so excited when I'm working on something that I can't wait to get back to the computer and polish it. I'll rewrite maybe thirty times, and then I know pretty much when a piece is done, and then I'll have to go through a new incubation. I sort of crash, and about three weeks later I'm charged up enough again to write another one, so I was doing one a month or a chapter a month. That seems to be my rhythm now, and it's working out nicely.

Does epilepsy work for you in the way that it worked for Dostoyevksy, where you have a heightened consciousness at points?

Yes. I had three of those experiences, and they were very profound. You never can forget them. But, basically, epilepsy is a total drag—I mean, the medicine you have to take. It's like taking rat poison; it's just nasty stuff, and I have to sleep a lot because of it. I really have to baby myself. My health isn't the greatest anymore.

Do you think you would have enjoyed being a witty doctor—kind of like Elliott Gould or Donald Sutherland in M.A.S.H.?

I think doctors are fascinating. A lot of doctors say, "You write like you're an insider. You really know what you're doing." And others say, "You know, you got this wrong," or, "You got that wrong," or whatever, but I have a lot of doctors who ultimately love my stuff. And I like writing about them, because I think the mystery of disease and so forth, it makes for good drama, just like the boxing stories do, or cowboy pictures do. You know, it's good versus evil; it's pretty simplistic stuff.

I'll continue to write about doctors. It's fun. And since our bodies are the only thing we can know, truly know, through them we can know the thing-in-itself, which is the universal.

What did you learn about life caring for your mother-in-law as she was dying from cancer?

My mother-in-law was a wonderful, very courageous person. She showed me courage. Getting into a boxing ring doesn't require that much courage. I think going to work every day and raising a family and being a moral human being requires courage. When she got the diagnosis, Tolstoy's *Death of Ivan Ilyich* came to mind, and I thought, *How can you wake up and go ten minutes without saying to yourself, "I've got cancer"?* Especially a person like me. I don't think I'd ever have a life—that would be the end—and so suddenly, although we always liked each other, once this happened, I was the only person that really could connect with her, that she could totally feel okay with. She wanted me around. I didn't say those crazy things that put walls up—and walls go up when you get a diagnosis like that— so we became great pals, and it was terrible to lose her, and I wanted to write that story ["I Want to Live"] to get even with the cancer. I got this in-your-face sort of voice because I was angry. I wanted to get even.

When I read your work, I'm reminded of two other humorous and diverse guys named Tom—McGuane and Boyle—and was wondering who you credit for developing your really strange and beautiful sense of humor?

Well, those guys are pretty good. In fact, I teach both at Iowa in my seminars. Being funny—I learned to be funny because I had a stepfather who would hit me whenever some dark thought floated into his brain. That's why I studied the art of self-defense. I knew someday I'd grow up and get big enough to get even with him, but being in the same room with him, I learned. And I think a lot of stand-up comics do it—to do anything to divert a bully, a frightening person. You make them laugh. I often realize how angry these comics are, and I don't know, I just always feel that since I did it this way, that's sort of a universal rule. That maybe it was the same with them, that they were funny because it was more of a survival mechanism. Funny people, Freud said, are usually the melancholics, the depressive types, for they see the absurdity of everything and they know the blackness of life, and I believe him very much. Freud's one of my great heroes.

Probably the funniest story in Cold Snap *is "Way Down Deep in the Jungle." It's a story about a man named Dr. Koestler, and he's getting a baboon drunk and stoned.*

Yes, I saw that happen. I noticed in the foreign-aid business that a lot of people are connected with missions, and they're really do-good types, and they're of that sort. But these doctors were more like the *M.A.S.H.* doctors were, but even darker, and I realized that a lot of them escaped from Australia, from Holland, from America, because they just don't fit in at home. And they're willing to put up with all the hardships of Africa simply so they can be themselves. And I watched these monkeys getting drunk, and I remember somebody saying there was a baboon that wouldn't drink because he had gotten into this colossal drunk, fell out of a tree, hurt his neck, and never touched another drop. But the monkeys would come back the next day and do it over again. They would do all the things humans do: there would be sex and then there would be fighting and then drunken remorse—Oh, God, I'm sorry, I'm sorry, man. You're my best friend. I'll never do that again. I love you, man. And then they vomit, and then they wake up in the morning and they're holding their heads in their hands, and then the whiskey comes out and they do it all over again. But the baboon learns. Once is enough.

The baboon's name is George Babbitt, reminiscent of Sinclair Lewis. You like to have these literary allusions layered in there. There's also a term that you use in that story: "a full Cleveland."

What does that mean?

A full Cleveland is your white-on-white tie; it's your polyester knit slacks, white patent leather shoes, white belt, and you could be a half Cleveland or you could go all the way with it.

So it's like painting your house museum beige all the time?

Yes, yes.

Tell us a little bit about the character, Ad Magic. He first appeared, dazed and confused, in The Pugilist at Rest. *Now he works for Global Aid in Africa, and I have to say I haven't met such a delightful con man since Rheinhardt, in Robert Stone's* A Hall of Mirrors. *What's he all about?*

Ad Magic is an alter ego. When I had the epilepsy, I would go off in these fugues, and I actually did end up in India one time, and didn't know how I got there. I had a hotel key; I didn't know which hotel, and I was in India, and it wasn't funny at all. I don't know how I got there. It was the strangest thing, and then it slowly came back to me. The horse was real. I sent money. I kept a horse alive for seven years. It was really interesting—I got to know the doctor in the story and the family, and I'm still in touch with them.

This is the story in The Pugilist at Rest?

I used him in "A White Horse" originally and got lots of mail asking me to please bring him back. People want to see the baboon again, too. I was out with my dog one day and some guy pulled up to me, and he said, "What happens to the monkey?" And I wondered what the hell he was talking about, and I looked at him and he said, "What happens to the baboon? Does the leopard get him or not?" I said, "Well, uh, I don't know," and that I hadn't thought about it, but a leopard probably would, and he said, "Don't do that! Don't do that! Keep him alive." So I said, "Okay, I'll keep him alive, you know, if it makes you happy and if I ever go back to it."

Ad Magic admits that he's been hallucinating for a lifetime, and he's kind of a drug-addled character in a way. I was wondering, you credited

102   *Glimmer Train Stories*

a couple of drug labs yourself for your skills as a writer, or your ability to maintain your consciousness while writing. You've taken a lot of heat for mentioning drug companies and giving them acknowledgments for the creation of Elavil and another drug—

Effexor. So good it feels illegal. Ooh, I like that one.

What have they done for you?

They make it possible to function. Elavil is sort of a baseline drug. I've been taking it since I was nineteen. It's a traditional antidepressant, and the one year I was off was the worst year of my life. I could not get out of bed; I couldn't choose between two loaves of bread without weeping.

You admit that you've used recreational drugs to excess as well.

Yes.

What did you learn during that period?

I'm not judgmental about drugs because people are simply taking drugs to feel normal. I mean, they're in pain, and America is a very violent, stressful place; and think of all the suicides that would have been if you couldn't once in a while have a drink or get stoned or something. Even animals like to do it, elephants and so on, baboons and monkeys—well, baboons, once. And so I did my share of that, because I was in great psychic pain. It wasn't like, hey, I decided one day I was going to grow up and be a drug addict, and go out and do horrible, shameful things, and get arrested, and go to detox and the nuthouse and so forth and so on—which did happen, and I did do; but once again, you can't erase your past.

You had the same kind of run-in with alcohol, but I understand you're stone-cold sober these days.

I haven't been stoned or drunk for ten years.

I really love the way you turn Australian strine into good effect in "Rocket Fire Red." You even turn the phrase "Come the raw prawn" into "Cometh the uncooked crustacean." I love that. Have you ever been to Australia?

Yes, yes, I love it there. I like New Zealand even better. They have such colorful ways of depicting some of these very essential acts of the human body and drinking and so on. It's very funny; I have an ear for that, of course, and it seems that sometimes I can just pass through a room and I've got a short story. And so when I was in Australia, I absorbed a lot of this stuff. I remember just as I was leaving for Iowa, I got a haircut, because it was very hot and I didn't have air conditioning in my Toyota, so I thought I'd get a really short haircut, and I went to this really cheap place, and the woman doing my hair was sort of overweight, and she had a depressing picture of a trailer and some sad-looking dogs, and I thought, *Let's cheer her up. I want her to feel better once I leave than she did before I came.* And I said, "Gee, that's beautiful hair you have. What color is that?" And she said, "It's called Rocket Fire Red." And right then I knew I had a story; I placed it in Alice Springs and Sydney. But that's how I get my stories. And I couldn't wait to get to Iowa, set up my computer, and write it, which I did, and that's how I got it, and it's only because I chose to be nice to this woman. I could have sat there and just endured the haircut and got out, because I wasn't feeling so great that day. I am glad I said that nice thing and God paid me off with a story.

Do you have the auditory counterpart to photographic memory?

Yes, yes. I retain a lot of stuff, particularly dialogue stuff.

There's a great line in "Dynamite Hands" [Cold Snap]—"You survived the bear's good information"—which in that story is an analog to Nietzsche's, "Whatever doesn't kill me makes me stronger." Are you a big believer in that dictum?

It depends on calibrations. If there's time to recover, sure, but an accumulation of blows can wipe you out. Nietzsche starts out as a Schopenhauerite and ultimately ends up as one, though it takes careful study, and that's just my opinion. I'd say, read it for yourself, and make of it what you will. But a bear chased me one time when I was running up a timber road in Washington State, and I remember I wasn't really frightened by it until it was over, and I could run six-minute miles in those days. And somehow these things work into your stories and you find them, and I know that I worked harder on that story probably than any other. The *New Yorker* first rejected it, then *Harper's* wanted me to rewrite it, but they didn't really give me tough enough instructions, and then *Playboy* got it and Alice Turner said, "This is what you need to do." And we went back and forth and back and forth, and it was a lot of fun. Alice locked in on the "boom boom" that's available from the universe, and how a fighter can accumulate energy, and how the bear was sort of a symbol of power; even though my narrator's going to lose for sure, he has to work—flog himself into this condition of self-delusion.

It seems to me that your characters are almost always hoisted up by their own petard, or their own canard, as it were. Does it seem to you that we humans take ourselves so seriously given our precarious position on the planet that we absolutely need to be made fun of?

Well, you know, if I didn't have a sense of humor ... it's the only thing that saves me. I do have a sense of the absurd, but I can get very serious about things. I can't speak for others because life is ... there is no such thing as a normal life, there's just life, and this is my life, and so I don't worry about a normal life. And I think it's true for everyone: there's just life. There's nothing to go running around to find. I tried, and it's right there, right in your own backyard. It's in you. Know thyself—if you can actually do that, pull that off, you begin to have a measure of peace.

Have you found a measure of peace through your writing?

Absolutely. When I write every day, I find a kind of wholeness and integration—psychic integration, and if I keep the schedule up it will sort of carry me the next day. It's the only way I can get high anymore. And I feel well; I feel okay about myself. Basically I've always hated myself, and I would do anything to escape "me." I suppose that's the reason I took drugs or would get into boxing. I subscribe to Schopenhauer's theory about how you lose yourself through art. You can transcend your own existence through art, and by creating art, too. I have to do it every day, but when I'm out on the road and whatnot, I start screaming at cab drivers or crazy things I still do, and I'm terribly ashamed of doing those things.

Are you driven by death fear, too, do you think?

Half of the time I wish I were never born, the other half I'm afraid I'm going to die. That's me.

When you charge up your own reading batteries, who do you turn to for sustenance?

Well, some of the writers we've already talked about. There are some books that I have around, perennial favorites, that if I pick them up, I'll start reading a line, and I'll have to read the whole book. You know, I might read it from the middle to the end, and then the beginning. I mean, I do that with *Dispatches,* I do it with *Dog Soldiers,* anything by Larry Brown. Reading for me was always the best thing, going to bed with a book at night is the best thing, like Somerset Maugham said. And when I read books that saved my life or came at the right time—all my life, I used to remember thinking, *Wow, whatever this person had to do to write this book or the price they had to pay*—and many of them paid some pretty big prices—I would think, *Thank God they did it! Thank God they did it! God bless 'em! If I could do that some day, that would be the most wonderful thing I could ever do.* And when I first read Dostoyevsky, there was probably no one that was more unlikely to become a writer than me, and yet somehow I did it, and I believe you can do it. I mean, I think the universe will come out and help you once you get yourself straight and get on the right road.

If you were to be abandoned alone in a cabin in the North Cascades for the rest of your life, and could only take along two books and one piece of music, which ones would you take?

Well, no surprises—I would take The Doors's double live cut of "Light My Fire," and I would take Schopenhauer to read.

Those are the ones I'd take; although if I wanted to get spiritual in this cabin, Franz Liszt and Brahms might do it. Does this cabin have cable and HBO? Are there fucking mosquitoes?

JIM SCHUMOCK interviews authors-on-tour for literary radio programs in Portland, Oregon. He is a major contributor to "Between the Covers" on KBOO and "Spotlight on Authors" on KBPS.

Noy Holland

This is me with my hair in a pixie, the year I
knocked out my tooth on a fencepost.

Noy Holland's short-story collection *The Spectacle of the Body* was published by Knopf last year. She is married to Sam Michel, a writer, who, she says: "keeps me happier than I likely seem in my work, and exceptionally well-fed." Holland and Michel spend much of their time in Massachusetts, where they are writers in residence at Phillips Academy. They also share a job teaching in the creative-writing program at the University of Florida. Holland and Michel have a bird dog, Alice, who was "born knowing how to unwrap presents, and to take down, gently, a woman's braided hair." Their first child was born in February 1996.

Noy Holland

Noy Holland
Someone Is Always Missing

*T*he baby was sleeping. The sisters had gone to the garden. There was flagstone around the garden. Lemon thyme bunched up between the slabs of stone. The dog lay down in the shade in the thyme and watched the girls in the garden.

The older sister said, "Listen for the baby, big dog."

It was the older sister's baby. It was the older sister's dog, the older sister's garden beside the older sister's house. The house was built in the sage and pine that grew on the slope of a hogback that tilted out of the plain. You could see across the plain from the garden.

"And these," the younger sister said, "are these keepers?"

The older sister, Celia, nodded. She knelt on the flagstone and pointed. It had been an easy birth. But it was hard still, bending. It was still hard for Celia to get herself around. "That's hearts-ease," she said, pointing. "There's motherwort and feverfew. This is hound's-tongue; here, rue. The rest of this is garbage."

The beds were dusty. The dust that lifted away from the plain and the chalky dust of the concrete plant covered every leaf and bloom. The sisters knocked the dust off as they weeded; they piled the weeds on the slabs of stone that Celia's husband had lain around the garden.

"I'm glad you came," Celia said to her sister.

The younger sister was Kate. She was the taller, the prettier one. She was the one their father kept moving from school to school. "Did you hear that?" Kate asked.

"What is it?"

"I thought I heard the baby."

Celia stopped and listened. She heard the wind moving the limbs of the trees and the dog, when it let its mouth drop open, breathing. But she couldn't hear the baby.

"Will Daddy come see the baby?" Kate asked.

"He says so. As soon as he can."

As Kate weeded, her shorts worked up until her underpants showed, the elastic, slack and useless. There were dusty streaks on the back of her shorts where she had wiped her hands.

"I mean it," Celia said. "I really am glad you came. It helps me, with the baby and all."

The dog rolled onto its back in the thyme. It showed the girls its body.

The days were getting hotter. The snowmelt was over, the runoff not plunging out of the mountains anymore.

The sisters moved on into the flowerbeds, into the bed where the iris was blooming. They had planted the iris the year before, not long after Celia was married, before the baby had begun to show. It was a year when winter came all at once. The girls had dug the new bed with a pickax in the falling snow, guessing at the borders of the older beds the new bulbs would bloom among. The bulbs had grown straight and healthy, sending up tall, strong stems whose blooms—this was why the sisters were digging them up now—were a murky, riverish brown.

Kate chipped the dirt up, twisted the spade to pry up the roots. "I'm so thirsty," she said. "All this digging."

"We'll be finished soon," Celia said. "If we go in, we'll wake the baby."

Kate dropped her spade, went to the hose, turned the faucet open, and drank until the water that had been left in the hose and been warmed by the sun ran out. Then she let the water, running cold, run out into the iris bed to make the bed easier to dig in.

"You can't do that," Celia said. "They won't let you water when it's dry like this."

"Who is 'they'?" Kate said.

"You know."

Kate turned off the faucet. She knelt again in the iris bed. "You know why *they* bring flowers to the hospital?" she said.

"Should I?" her sister said.

"It's so they don't have to smell you."

Kate leaned into the stand of blooms. She dipped her nose between the petals of one of the blooms.

It surprised her, it had always surprised her—that the bulbs knew when to grow. All those months in the ground in the snow, she thought, and remembered that, the year before, the snow had already begun falling. Kate had been between schools. It was the year she had dropped a cigarette into a pile of dirty clothes and burned down her apartment. Their father had sent her out. He sent her to Celia with a dachshund, which Celia gave away, and with a shopping bag full of iris bulbs which he guessed, in his note, were tulips. *At the very least,* the note read, *these should keep your sister out of harm's way.*

Celia said, "They teach you that in school, I guess."

"I guess so."

Kate tossed a muddy clump she had pulled free onto the pile of weeds on the flagstone. Celia squatted behind her. She picked the iris up by the handful, and the weeds, loading her arms from the top of the pile. She saw the nubs of Kate's spine underneath her shirt, poking out from her curving back. Kate was thin, thinner than Celia had seen her get, boyish and hard. Celia, this soon after the baby, felt thick and slow and swelled still. She squatted until her knees hurt and then stood up slowly behind her sister and said to the back of her head, "You didn't have to go through with it. Nobody made you."

"You would know, of course."

"I'm just saying, Kate."

Kate went on digging. "You know what's funny?" she said to her sister. "They don't even have to talk to you. They just stand around near the door." She wiped her mouth with the arm of her shirt. "They took turns," she said. "When Jack got tired, Daddy came limping up the hall. Don't you think that's funny?"

"And what did they say?" Celia said.

"Nothing. They just stood there. I'd be in bed, reading, filing my nails, whatever, and I'd hear them. Jack came over every day; I kept thinking he would give up and say something, or that Daddy would, you know, a word, my name, whatever. One of them or the other. I thought once that maybe one of them might come in and sit on the bed. God."

She jabbed around in the hole she had dug with the dented tip of her spade.

"They must have said something," Celia said.

"Sure, like, 'Honey, it's nothing.' Something like that?" Kate said.

"Forget it."

"'All they have to do is go up in there and squirt a little—'"

"I said forget it," Celia said.

"I mean weeks of it. God," she said. "Them standing around in the hall out there eating gingersnaps." Kate looked up at her sister. She saw her sister not seeing her, not looking. "Don't you see?" she said.

"Not really."

"Really?" Kate insisted.

"I don't. I don't understand you. I don't see why you had to wait so long so you had to even go to the hospital and actually have to *have* the thing." She was walking across the flagstone. "It's unreasonable. It's just a lot of moaning."

Celia walked around behind the house. She dropped the armload of iris and weeds on the heap of limbs and clippings and scratched around on the head of the dog, who followed wherever she went now and was standing at her knee. She listened for the baby. She climbed onto a stack of concrete blocks and looked through the high window. The baby was still asleep. The dog was standing behind Celia, whining, getting ready to spring up onto the blocks. Kate was calling the dog from the garden. The telephone was ringing. Celia listened for Kate to go into the house and wake up the baby to answer the phone. But the phone kept ringing. Kate kept calling the dog from the garden. Celia watched the baby until the ringing stopped. The baby was still asleep when it stopped.

When Celia came back to the garden, Kate said, "That was Jack, I guess."

"What makes you say so?"

"Because I know him," Kate said. "He was calling to make sure I got here. He always does that."

"Well, that's good," Celia said.

"Do you think so?"

"Kate."

"He called the hospital, too. Isn't that good? He sent a big bunch of flowers."

Celia went back to digging, piling up the iris. A cluster of low, unimpressive clouds was being blown across the plain. A truck turned off the asphalt road and began to throw from the slope of sage the powdery trail of dust that rose, and drifted, thinning, behind it.

"Ah," Kate said, "the man of the house."

She walked out onto the driveway and waved at him as he came.

Celia threw together an easy meal while her husband played with the baby. He passed brightly colored rings above the baby's face, fingered it under its chin. The baby's eyes were barely open. Its skull was still a funny shape, squeezed into a pointy hump at the back of the head.

Celia's husband put the baby in a wicker basket and set the basket on the floor at his feet when it was time to come to the table. The dog lay down near the basket, watching the baby, lifting up its head from between its paws whenever the baby moved at all or made the slightest sound.

"What a good dog," Kate said.

It lifted its head to let her pat it.

Celia's husband ate without speaking. When Kate twisted around to re-tie the robe she had come to dinner in, Celia's husband kept his eyes on his plate. When he had finished eating all the food on his plate, he picked the plate up and licked it, and when he put the plate down again, there were pieces of food in his beard. He had a sprawling, sunburnt beard and a lumpy, porous nose. His mouth was completely grown over. When he spoke to the baby, all you saw of his mouth was a neat row of tiny teeth and the tip of his tongue between them.

"Blauwgh," he said, "goochy goo. Talk to Big Bear, Baby."

He rocked the basket roughly and the baby sloshed side to side.

"Go easy," Celia said.

The baby had to wear a foamy tube strapped around its leg, to brace it. The leg had caught on something, some bone or cord or who knew what; it had been twisted around and broken in Celia while the baby was being born. The tendons and ligaments of the knee were torn so that the leg, the foot—it was better now, Celia knew it was getting better—but it had been something to see, the way it flopped around when the brace was off. With the brace off, the leg had looked detachable, like the limb of a plastic doll.

Celia cleared the table. She came around behind her husband and picked the pieces of food from his beard.

Kate brushed the dander from his shirt sleeve. The dog got up, whining, and walked underneath the table. Kate listened to it

114   *Glimmer Train Stories*

sniffling. She felt it rub up against her leg. She unwrapped the piece of chewed-up meat she had spat out into her napkin and held the meat in her hand.

"You better quit that," Celia's husband said. "I asked her not to do that."

"Do what?" Celia said.

Celia's husband kicked at the dog underneath the table.

"I'm just sitting here," Kate said.

"You're not," said the husband. "Goddamnit. I asked you not to do that."

"Do what?" Celia said.

Kate pushed away from the table. She held the meat out between the slats of her chair where the dog could see it behind her. The dog took a step, slowly, as though it were having to step across something that hurt its paws. It was looking up at the husband.

"Do you want that?" the husband said to the dog.

Kate dropped the meat into the pocket of her robe.

The husband stood up. "You want that?"

The dog sat down behind Kate's chair, pretending to be yawning.

"I thought so," he said.

"That's a good dog," he said, and walked over to the dog to pat it. He walked to the basket, the baby in the basket, and carried it away from the table.

"Here you go," he said to his wife.

Celia saw, from his eyes, that he was grinning, and from his ears, which had moved a little ways up the sides of his head.

He went out of the house with a hammer and saw, and with nails poking out of his pockets. He cut a few boards for the soffit, and stepped up the ladder with one of the boards and with nails sticking out of his mouth. He held the board against the joists with his shoulder. Swallows built nests in the eaves. Clots of mud from the nests they built were spattered against the side of the house; mud was dried on the screens of the windows.

When he banged on the house, the dog barked. Kate broke a glass on the faucet. She picked the pieces up, dropped them into the bottom of the glass, and dropped the glass in the garbage. She rinsed the sink out, and filled it up again.

The wind was quitting. The boat was bottom-up in the yard.

Celia turned on the water in the bathroom. Kate saw the dog go into the bathroom, and she heard it drink from the toilet bowl. Kate didn't wash the husband's—she didn't wash Big Bear's plate. Instead, she wiped off the flowery rim where Big Bear hadn't quite licked it clean and she set the plate down in the dish rack. The rest of the plates, she scraped and stacked and left in the soapy water. Then Kate walked down the hall to the bathroom. The dog was curled up on the bathmat.

Celia took her clothes off. She took the baby's little jumpsuit off, the baby's little foamy brace. The baby's skin was chaffed underneath the brace, and flaking. Celia scraped off some of the flaked-up skin with the squarish nail of her thumb. She shut the faucet off and stepped into the tub, holding the baby against her. Its thin, bowed legs, when she sat down, hung between her own legs. She dipped the baby into the water.

Kate put the top down on the toilet bowl and sat on it to watch. She scratched behind the dog's ears as she watched. The mirror rattled, and little ripples came up in the water in the tub whenever Big Bear drove a nail into the eaves with his hammer. He was working his way toward the bathroom, stopping to cut the soffit boards and then hitting in nails again.

"Here," Kate said, "I can help you."

Kate washed her sister's back for her, soaping it up and then rinsing it with a cup she had brought from the kitchen. Her sister's skin had gotten smoother. Her hair had gotten thicker, shinier than it used to be. Her breasts were bigger than Kate's now. Kate slipped her hand under her sister's arm, turning the soap in her armpit. She moved the soap over her sister's ribs, which used to show underneath her skin. Celia lifted the baby away from her chest and held it propped against her legs, holding her arms away from her sides to let her sister wash her. Kate soaped up Celia's belly, her breasts, her nipples, cracked and lumpy. She pushed into her nipple with the ball of her thumb. A little milk came out.

Celia felt her sister's hands shake.

"Kate, Kate," Celia said.

Kate had started very quietly crying. "I kept thinking if I waited another day I would feel it move," she said. "I wanted to feel it, what that feels like. I know it's stupid."

Celia kissed her sister's fingers. She handed her sister the baby.

Celia let Kate wash the baby—its bottom, its skinny legs, its little curling feet. She let Kate lather the dark hair whorled on the baby's funny head, Kate keeping the soap away from its face the way Celia had shown her. The baby jerked its little arms around. It poked out the little white callus on its lip it already had from sucking.

"Look," Celia said. "She likes it."

She stepped out of the tub to give them room and pulled a towel off the towel rack.

Celia's husband ran a saw through a board. He stepped up onto the ladder. With the claw of his hammer he scraped at the mud that was left of the nests the swallows made.

Celia swung her hair up, over her head, to dry it.

Kate dipped the baby's head in the water. She turned the baby onto its belly, held it there, let go. The dog got up, barking. The baby started to swim. Only its little bottom, and the pointy hump at the back of its head, stuck up out of the water. The baby lunged—jerky, froggish—paused, trailing its little crooked leg; it swam over half the length of the tub before Celia saw what her sister had done and knocked past her, screaming, and snatched the baby out of the water.

"What are you doing?" Celia screamed. She held the baby against her. The baby was quiet. She hit her sister across the mouth. "What did you think you were doing?"

"She was swimming," Kate said. "She liked it."

It was true that the baby was quiet. Its little mouth was open, it was waving its little hands—a baby newly enough from the womb that it could still do that, hold its breath and swim like that. It had not forgotten yet how to do that.

When it was dark outside and the wind had quit and the baby was in its crib asleep, Celia's husband came in. Kate heard him, heavy-footed, walk down the hall with his toolbox.

She tried to get the dog to sleep with her, tried to trap it underneath the covers. Kate patted the sheet, and tugged on the dog's collar, but the dog, when it jumped on the bed at all, only jumped right off again. She gave up. She swung the door shut to keep the dog in her room, and flipped the light off.

The beds—the one that Kate was in, and the one where Celia and her husband slept—were side by side, pushed against opposite sides of the wall. Kate listened through the wall for them. She waited until they were quiet, until Celia and her husband seemed to be asleep, and then she went in to look at the baby. The baby was sleeping. It was making little sleeping sounds. The dog sat beside Kate and whimpered.

She went into the kitchen. She got Big Bear's plate from the dish rack and toasted four frozen waffles, heaped them with ice cream and chocolate sauce, and ate them in the dark in bed. She let the dog lick the plate when she had finished. This time, when she patted the covers, the dog jumped up in the bed.

118

She dreamed: they were with the dog, she and Celia, in the mountains. There was snow still, in patches, and moss that grew over their knees. In the snow was an overturned pickup truck she and Celia climbed out of. Their clothes were torn. They looked for wounds, for broken bones. They found the baby— not Celia's baby, but the tiny thing that Kate felt drop into the toilet in the hospital—beginning to grow on her tongue.

Kate woke up, and Celia and the dog and the baby woke up, all at once before the sun: Big Bear had burned his toast. The dog got up. Kate lay in bed, listening, remembering she had turned the toaster up to toast her frozen Eggos. She pulled her robe on, and let the dog out. She stood in the doorway, watching the dog following its nose in the light from the house.

It was dark still; the wind had not started to blow. Smoke was rising in columns from the concrete plant and drifting out over the plain, over a band of cottonwoods that bent over a path of stones that had once been the bed of a river.

The boat was gleaming, bottom-up in the grass in the yard.

Kate tried to remember her dream. She remembered, instead, that she walked in her sleep for years before she moved from home, when home was a lush, dampened place, a county of hills and fences. In her sleep, she buried her family's shoes in the sawdust pile beside the barn. She woke herself in shopping malls, on roadways, in neighbors' yards—in places, some nights, she had never been and did not know how to go home from. One night she woke up lying in a dew, in grass so tall she saw only leaves, threaded and sharp, and limpid stems, nodding their frayed heads. Something was eating toward her: she had fallen asleep in a field of cows. When a few of them found her, others came. They stood above her, flank to flank, wide, wet, eyelashy eyes and dished cow faces, waiting to see what she would do.

She went in to look at the baby. "Hey, pretty girl. What you doing?" she said.

She shook the crib for the baby. She pinched a piece of lint from its mouth.

"Mkgnao," she said. "Hulululu. Wakey, wakey, baby."

The baby lay there. She picked it up, cradling its head the way she remembered seeing her sister do. She remembered the place where the bone hadn't met on the top of the baby's head, the dent you could press your thumb against and count the heart-beats through.

She counted to twelve, or seven, and started to count again.

When they were five and six, the girls, of an age for dolls, loved the same blonde, limbless thing until a day they fed it, set it to sit in the highchair where the girls themselves had used to sit, with the spoon they had learned to eat from. When Kate pulled the doll's hair to bend its neck back to dribble ice cream into its mouth, the doll's eyeballs had dropped from their sockets and fallen back into its head. It was something she had nearly forgotten.

Kate remembered, as a rule, very little.

A sheepdog drowned in the swimming pool in the year her hair was pixied.

She remembered her hair in a pixie.

She remembered a moose with removable wounds, meaty pieces you could lift out and put back in again.

Kate carried the baby out through the garden, feeling in her feet—her feet were bare—how the ground dipped and cooled in the beds, dampish where she had run the hose where she and Celia had dug up the iris.

She called, "Here, boy. C'mere, boy."

The dog came to her, smelling of sage, and walked along at her heels. They walked across the flagstone, and over the brittle, golden grass.

Where the grass stopped, the hogback began to slope away. At the foot of the slope were heaps of slag that grew, year by year, beside the concrete plant. A few lights went off in the concrete plant.

The baby fumbled at her, hungry.

"Are you hungry?" she said.

The dog whimpered.

"Not you," she said to the dog. But the dog bucked and jumped at her feet to show that it was hungry. It trotted back to the house with its nose to the ground, looking for its bowl.

Kate pulled her robe across the baby. She started down over the hogback. Goatheads grew on the hogback, low along the ground. They had pale stems, narrow leaves you never seemed to see until you had walked into a patch of them, which is what Kate did. She tried walking first on the sides of her feet, where the skin was thick, and then on tiptoe. She tried stopping and standing on one foot to pull a few thorns from the other foot, feeling with her fingers for the thorns that had worked into the tenderest places. But the baby cried when she bent at the stomach, and the thorns on the foot she was standing on pushed in even deeper.

She went on. Behind her, a door squeaked open. The dog arrived with its bowl in its mouth and, picking its way among the thorns, walked along with her down the hill.

She was walking to a flat stone she remembered having sat on. The stone had been painted white, and the air around it looked lighter. It looked bigger, the stone, than it really was, as big to her as a smallish boat moored against the heaps of slag the chalky dust blew off of. The dust was in her mouth, her eyes; she couldn't see quite. She saw the rim of the plain grow lighter, and the stone seemed to move away.

The dog dropped the bowl in the path they had walked, and walked to the stone to watch her. She remembered the meat in her pocket. She had Big Bear's fork in her pocket.

"Watch me," she said to the dog. She walked into a patch of cactus, a cluster of pale, puffy crowns whose spines broke off in her arches.

She sang, "Baby, baby."

Her sister appeared in the light from the house and held her hands over the rim of the hill.

Kate took the baby's brace off, tossed it over her shoulder. She tossed the meat down the hill to the dog. She stamped around in the cactus. But then she couldn't think what else to do.

The wind had begun to blow as it does when day begins in this part of the world. Kate's robe was flapping open. The baby was sucking at her, a bony, gummy mouth.

Celia called out.

Kate heard her; she could barely hear her.

She was thinking of the baby against her, how small she was, and silky, and creased, and round. She thought the baby would weep soon. It would look up and speak her name.

Kate found she was counting heartbeats. She was thinking she could feel her heart beat as you can sometimes in your fingertips, behind your knees, in your teeth sometimes. She could feel that. But she could not keep up, counting—it was too fast, thready, the ragged shallow quickening pulse not of her own heart, she realized, but of the baby's heart, the dent on the top of the baby's head twitching against her arm. Her arm felt weak and tingly.

She couldn't see quite, she thought she saw him, coming over the yard in his boxer shorts.

He came over the yard in his boxer shorts. He had hair all over his body.

Kate felt herself starting to pee, or bleed. She saw him start down over the hogback and she squatted with the baby in the dust as he came. She felt the shudder he caused in the ground as he came, in her knees, in the bones of her hands—she swore that she could feel that—a blunt heavy bear of a man running down to her through the cactus, the goatheads, his wide, flat feet winging out.

Barbara Scot

Barbara Scot

Untangling the threads

Interview

by Linda Davies

Barbara Scot, born Barbara Norris, grew up on a farm in
Scotch Grove, Iowa, with her
brother, her mother, and her
mother's mother. Neither a Presbyterian nor a Scot, Barbara is a
naturalist and a historian, so when
she decided to try to make sense of
her own life, she went back to the
comprehensive records of the Scotch
Grove Presbyterian Church. In
Prairie Reunion *(Farrar, Straus
and Giroux), we follow her discovery of the history of the land, the
community, and her place in it.*

Barbara Scot

Scot is also the author of **The Violet Shyness of their Eyes:
Notes from Nepal** *(Calyx Books, 1993). A former high-school
teacher, she spends her time now researching and writing.
Portland has been her home for over twenty years.*

DAVIES: *You were very revealing in* Prairie Reunion.
SCOT: You know, I wasn't until the fifth draft.
  Why was that?
  Well, in writing the book, I lived through all that psycho-

logical unraveling and discovery. I just hadn't planned to share it completely with the reader, but I was on my fourth draft when I found my agent and she said, *This is very good, I'm quite sure I can sell it, but this needs more of your pain.* I knew she was right— what would make this a marketable book would be to use my own pain because this is what people would most identify with. But I felt like I'd already sold the bones of my ancestors and now I was going to sell my own soul as well, and when this first started being billed as a memoir, it was rather disturbing to me. *I considered the main focus to be social history, using a family as a vehicle to work through social history.* So it was distressing that everything capitalized on my personal story. And if this was anyone's memoir, I felt it was my mother's. She was a very private person. I had nightly discussions with her: *Mom, it's not just our story, I'm not really telling your story, I'm telling the story of women at a particular time. I'm telling social history, the fracture of the strong patriarchal family. It's not just your story,* but I *was* using her story. Now I see it really is mine as well. And the more I studied her little note, I thought she was giving me permission.

That note! How she could leave that as her last set of words to you was just astonishing to me. It demands a follow-up conversation—which you cannot have! [Barbara's mother is long dead.] What do you think she was thinking when she did that?

When you work through someone else's pain, it gives you the possibility of more joy in your own life and I think that note was my mother's last gift, that she deliberately constructed this puzzle because she knew for me to work through it would liberate me. And it did.

Maybe we should say what this book is about for those readers who haven't read it yet.

It's about unraveling the threads that have tangled up your immediate family and yourself and reconnecting to more positive eternal strands. I started with a family mystery which was my mother's undying loyalty to my father who had left her with two small children, a mountain of debts, a mortgaged farm, a humiliating situation in a small farming community in eastern Iowa in the 1940s—he ran away with the neighbor's wife. Seven years later, in a nearby area, he committed suicide. She never spoke ill of him.

Although she was a school teacher with a four-year college degree, she returned to her childhood home, our ancestral farmhouse—my grandfather, who was dead by then, had amassed twelve hundred acres in the area—to live with my grandmother, and she raised us on this farm. She only taught a few years until the country schools were closed. And we grew up there in a very silent house. The farm was run by my uncle Jim, who lived just up the road with his family.

Ten years before I started writing, I had returned after a long, long absence, and found a trunk of my things that my mother had left for me, and in there was a box of letters—the letters were relatives' letters to her and first drafts of her letters, and they detailed the story of her brief, unhappy marriage—and this very mysterious note with the three puzzling lines: *What do you think? You don't understand. You'll never know how much.* They were all wrapped in her wedding dress.

I waited ten years before I tackled it; then I went back and stayed at the farmhouse again myself, the farmhouse of my childhood, of her childhood, which now is a bed and breakfast ironically named Sweet Memories. It's run by my cousin, a fact I never could have made up. And I spent quite a bit of time there figuring out these puzzles.

You did a great deal of research. There is a lot of history in this book.

As a historian, it saddens me that more of it couldn't have been included. I could have filled my first draft with footnotes; I found out so much about the area. I was trying to understand my mother, and then I had to understand my father, the man she'd loved, and to understand them, I had to understand the Scotch Grove Presbyterian Church that was the basis of the community for all of us. That turned out to be such an experience. Their thoroughly intact records go back to 1887, which is not that unusual. I highly recommend anyone, whether they're interested in their own family history or history of place, to check into their little church records. It's just amazing what is there. Now you would have to raid psychiatrists' offices to get what I found out in that church. It was wonderful. That was when I understood that I had this little kernel of social history.

Why is history so irresistible to you?

Because we are so much a part of it. To understand ourselves— well, take immediate history, the sins of my father: they were simply a repetition of earlier sins. Rather than magnify them, it minimized them. It was just part of the human condition. Something that societies had been struggling with for a long time. Every major crisis I had faced myself as an adult— the dissolution of my first marriage, the issue of abortion—had already been dealt with in the church, and I understood so much more. And when I got farther back into the native history of the area, and realized that all of us were these little streams of humanity flowing over the land, it took some of the edge off the environmental diatribe I'd started with. I really do a lot with nature, so I should have known more than I did, but you know how, as a child, you always thought the buffalo were farther west. You think the destruction is not as connected to you as it turns out to be when you actually read the exact history of your place, what your ancestors were part of. I came to understand that it had a whole lot to do with me and with them and with that place. But I also came to understand—and it's not an excuse for the total obliteration of a species, or for completely altering the tall-grass prairie, or for having no sense of preservation of ways of life—that nature is bigger than all of us. We are just this little tidepool between limestone bluffs of earlier seas. As I said, it doesn't exonerate us for anything, but it gives you a great, or it gave me a great faith in the restorative powers of nature itself, in the strength of the land. And that's why history is so important.

So you gained tremendous perspective! It must have been a relief to discover that you and your family and your family situation were not singularly dreadful.

Oh, exactly. I even ended up thinking my relatives were pretty nice! Not only did I not resent them, I felt so tender toward, for example, my father. Again, this is not the same as exonerating him for what he did to my mother, to his children—all five of them that he sired by the time he was done—but I could see that this young man of thirty-seven years had killed himself because he had been unable to untangle these cords that had impressed their pattern on him. And old Gideon Hughes, this grandfather that all of my life I had resented because we didn't have curtains at the windows—I came to understand that my grandmother actually had a lot of money; even after he was dead, she just could not bring herself to spend any of it because she didn't consider it hers. You see that all the time, or you used to, anyway, that women would think you shouldn't waste your husband's money. And that's the way she felt. It can place an incredible burden on you if you do not feel part of the process, if you do not feel that your contribution is valued. So even after my grandfather died, she could not touch that money. She patched her stockings.

Flashbacks are difficult: easily confusing or contrived feeling. Yours were handled quite gracefully even though they went back sometimes to childhood, sometimes to adult psychiatric sessions.

Well, thank you. That's a very hard thing to pull off. It may have worked more successfully for you than for some people because I think it is an element of difficulty in the book. But when you go back to the place where you were as a child—and I encourage anyone to try this—you see part of it with twelve-year-old eyes and part of it with six-year-old eyes, and part of it as an adult looking back, and these layers are all happening at the same time. To transcribe that is a tremendous challenge. At first, I played around a whole lot with italics and visual clues and things like this. That's one way that [my editor] Jonathan Galassi really helped me. He just said, *Cut them all out.* And I did. He said, *Your readers are more intelligent than this. They will figure it out; give them more credit.* He was right, I think. But it is demanding at times for the reader because you're going along happily thinking you're at one point in time and then suddenly there's a shift of voice.

Those segments with a psychiatrist were the most metaphoric parts in the book because I really only went to the psychiatrist a short time. I had to combine that with what I had actually done in my own head—I did a lot of this by journaling—and present them as little episodic conversations. I wrote those seven pieces that are the psychiatric thread in a week and a half, then I spread the manuscript over my whole upstairs and I placed them, pulling in threads here and there to try to weave it all in. And I knew I had it then.

Did you originally plan to write about this whole thing?

No, although I thought that I had a book. Actually, that's a bit of a fudge; I knew I had a book. I just didn't know quite what the book was. In fact, I knew that I had a book to the point that I quit my teaching job to write. That was a major step and decision, and if I hadn't have been able to count on my husband's support in this, it would have been an incredibly dangerous step to take. But it's like this book has had a life of its own and my position has been finding the story. I knew the story was there, I knew it was going to get written. I knew that it was going to get published, which is a very arrogant thing to say in this publishing world, but I knew this was going to go. And when Jean [my agent] took this book back to New York, we had four bids on it, major bids. It was an incredible thrill. Especially to an unemployed school teacher; I haven't firmly identified myself as a writer yet. I had this amazing discussion with one woman who had bid on the book who said, *You know, not to use Presbyterian terms, but this book seems to have a strange kind of predestination, and I think that you will choose where you should be* [which publisher should take *Prairie*]; *you will choose the right one.* It was very interesting. And I felt that all along: that this story is more than my own. I don't want to use a word like channeling, but I think that at certain times it's almost as if combinations of intelligence come together for you. I'm dealing in a sense with my mother's mind, with that community mind, and partly with the land itself. My role was almost translator and combiner, and I had to be very careful and respectful of everything that I was dealing with. And I'm experiencing that even more so now, with a project that came out of this.

What is that?

When I was researching the Scotch Grove Presbyterian Church, I encountered a one-line reference to a communion cup. The early Scots, who'd been evicted from the Highlands, had, over twenty-three years, come to the Red River colony that became Winnipeg, and ultimately came down this ox-cart trail to eastern Iowa—a thousand miles—and they brought a communion cup with them the whole way. I didn't follow that up at that time, but I didn't forget that line, and all of a sudden one night, after I sold *Prairie,* I woke in the middle of the night, thinking about that cup: *Where did I see that? Did I really see a line that said that? Is there really a cup? Is it still there?* So I went back to Scotch Grove, Iowa, and found the cup, and got permission to take it, and I am now recreating the journey of these Scots. And I feel like I am just a vehicle for finding this story which is so representative of migration of peoples, of exiles, of community. These were Highland Scots way, way up north, Southerlandshire, in this little parish of Kildonan. I've gone over there, and I went to the very church which is now in a sheep pasture and took the cup back to the very pulpit where the eviction notices were read. I found the exact people in a memoir. It's amazing. Now what I'm doing is that I'm carrying the cup on the whole journey. I'm starting in April. And at the end of this, I'm going to incorporate the people from that church and community with the elders that I still know.

My impression from reading so much about your mother is that she'd be thrilled with your being so adventurous. She clearly was a rather playful person who liked fun and adventure a lot.

Even though she never got to have much of it. She had a large internal world that compensated for a small external world. I've been very fortunate in having a lot of external adventures. I've gone a lot of places and done a lot of things. In one article they said, *Well, what's the difference between a memoir and an autobiography?* And I said that in an autobiography, I would have talked about backpacking in Peru and climbing in the Himalayas.

What caveats or suggestions would you offer to people thinking about writing autobiographical material to present to the world?

Nothing is irrelevant. The strongest temptation is to think, *Oh, but they wouldn't be interested in that.* But the most ordinary parts of our lives are the very things that tie us to the human condition. There's such an emphasis now on the spectacular. Did you read that article in *Time?* [Week of October 16, 1995.] It's a bizarre article—though what they said about me was perfectly fair and true—about confessional memoirs. When Farrar, Straus told me I was going to be in this, I said, *Confessional memoirs! At least I would have talked about the sex I had instead of the sex I didn't have. How can this be a confessional memoir?* In the piece itself, they draw readers in by capitalizing on the bizarre things, like there's one section about murders, one about incest—all of these things happen and probably do need to be talked about, I'm not minimizing that at all as a release for people. But I am saying that that which is the most ordinary is that which unites you with other people. The detail of tenderness or pain. It's so ordinary. We're tempted not to use it because it seems like we're being sentimental. This book's only been out a short while, but I've had people writing and calling, and when they say this or that

130

touched them, it moves me. I'm rather interested in hearing other people's stories back. I think that's what you have to do, if you're going to tell your story, is to listen to the stories of others. The things they mention that touched them are so common. So very common. There are things like, *Well, my father left the family and no one ever said anything about it,* but the common element is the silence, the silence about shame. That's not something that was just one generation.

I wonder if all the talk shows are a purging for all the silence, a swing in the opposite direction, so that we can eventually come to some kind of dignified and open place.

That might be true, although I think in a situation like that where people get only one moment of exposure—I think people get fixated on a revelation like that and they tell it and tell it and tell it, and you know, I think, *Oh, there's so much more to it than that.* It's such a process to get to the stuff.

I really feel I attained adulthood in that one moment when I went from feeling like a child deprived of her father to a prodigal who hadn't realized how much Uncle Jim had really been a father to her. The essential step is from concentrating on what you were—or imagined you were—deprived of, and understanding what you were given. I did not make that leap until the very end of the writing process.

So the writing itself allowed you to make some sense of it?

Oh, yes, yes. Back to your question about autobiographical writing, I think that's perhaps the essential benefit of the writing. It really doesn't have to do with whether it will be published. I mean, I think we all write to be published, we want to be heard, we want to share what we have created, but internally there will be a great deal of value for you in dealing with your autobiographical material in writing.

I am curious whether you have a desire or expect to have a desire to reconnect with your brother.

I could connect with him, of course. I know his ex-wife well,

I know his children, but I really meant it when I said in the book that he has a right not to be found and I think it is important to respect that even though people are biologically tied to us, they do not have to answer to us. I think we all have relatives that we would like to work things out with, dead or alive, and it's much easier with the ones who are dead and hold still. The ones who are alive have their own realities. I think of talking to my mother now and having her say, *Well, that wasn't quite the way it was.* I've got it all worked out, but she'd want to argue about it or something.

You once had the good fortune to overhear your mother say, She's my pride and joy. *I thought that was marvelous. I wondered, when does that memory come to mind for you?*

Actually, I think I just carry it in my mind. I heard her say that to Esther Sinclair on the phone. It was wonderful. It was incredibly important to me. Especially growing up in a world where you thought that the men were more valued than you. You thought that your brother was more important because he was the boy. You thought that the farms depended on the men and that you couldn't even help in the barn with your little housebroom. That's what I meant by an insignificant detail, by the way, the most ordinary details. Who would ever be interested in the fact that I tried to sweep the cobwebs off the ceiling of the barn and that my uncle Jim told me to go back in the house?

Is there one person now in your life by whom you feel most truly known?

I, of course, would probably say my husband or my sons, but that's not true. My husband knows a lot about me, but not about the writing part. He's proud and very supportive, but he's just not involved in that part of my life at all. And my kids are in their twenties, they're very busy with their own lives, and I love my sons dearly, but there are parts of your life that you really don't— maybe you'll have a nice discussion the way my mother did with me, or maybe you'll leave it in a trunk, but you still won't tell them the whole story. I have a friend that I mention in the book as my soul sister, and I really think she knows me best. I don't deal with a large group of friends; I just mostly go out and watch birds and stuff, and take my dogs to the river. I have another friend who knows more about me than anyone else; I only see her infrequently, but I could go to her at any time and say, *I gotta tell you something.* And there's the woman I run with. I'm very fortunate that way to have a few very close, dear friends.

No one person can know all of someone, I don't suppose, but it seems important to have those chunks of you known somehow.

But we've all had to do without that at times; we all know that kind of loneliness, and I think for men, it's been much, much harder. It was so important for me to recognize, as I wrote this book, that life was not easier for men. This book's not about anything original. All of the truths that I achieved in it are very simple, easy ones. Such ordinary truths.

Gary D. Wilson

Look closely (I'm the ten- or eleven-year-old on the right) and you can tell how much I loved fishing, or at least the result of it. Note the curled left hand and the proud, secure grip I have on the fish—the delight on my face. I think the only joy I had in posing for this picture was that for some reason I got to hold the big fish and my brother didn't, which nearly made it worthwhile.

Gary D. Wilson's fiction has appeared in numerous publications, including *Quarterly West*, Baltimore's *City Paper*, *The William and Mary Review*, *Witness*, *Kansas Quarterly*, *Wisconsin Review*, *Nimrod*, *Sun Dog*, *Amelia*, *Outerbridge*, *Descant*, *Quartet*, *Green's Magazine*, *Cottonwood Review*, *Itinerary* (now *Mid-American Review*), and *Glimmer Train Stories*. He currently has a novel and a collection of stories making the rounds.

Wilson, who is married and has two sons, teaches fiction workshops at Johns Hopkins University and also works part-time at a Baltimore public middle school, where he teaches creative writing and co-directs The Write Place, the school's writing center. He was born and reared in Kansas, and earned an MFA from Bowling Green State University, Ohio, where he studied under Philip F. O'Connor. He has taught at various colleges and universities in the U.S., and spent two years teaching high-school English for the Peace Corps in Swaziland, Africa.

GARY D. WILSON
A Middle-Aged Man

Takes stock

Out the door, down the steps. Warm, blue sky, birds chirping, grass sprouting, forsythia set to explode. He should be happy, but he isn't, and it worries him. The darkness that has settled over him, enveloped him, has become his constant and most intimate companion. In general, he has learned to accommodate himself to it. No one at work knows, and only on rare, unguarded occasions at home does his wife ask, "What's wrong?" or, "Is something the matter?" To which he invariably answers no, because nothing is that he can name and therefore talk about. He has no pain. He has no scar. He isn't blind or lame or otherwise impaired. To everyone concerned, he seems perfectly normal and well-adjusted.

Which he is, in the usual sense. He isn't brutal or abusive. He doesn't use drugs. He doesn't smoke, and drinks only modestly. He doesn't ever intentionally expose himself to anyone. He doesn't make a habit of peeking in other people's windows or reading other people's mail. To him, Madonna is more shrewd whore than entertainer. Maybe that's all any of them are in the end, though, he reasons—shrewd whores who sell whatever they have to the highest bidder.

But that's a hell of an attitude to pass on to his children. He should do something about it.

Examines himself

Naked as the day he was born, he opens the closet door and

looks long and hard at himself in the full-length mirror. Front, side, back as far as he can see. Upside down between his legs. Gut sucked in, pooched out. Any uglier, and with a bit more of a slouch, he could pass for a great ape. He's definitely hairy enough—except on his head, which is okay, because apes are bald too. Only he'll have to be a silverback, since there isn't enough dark fur left to qualify him for anything else. He leans forward, dangling his arms and head, swings one hand up to his pit and scratches, makes what he thinks are ape noises, straightens up his jowls with the backsides of his fingers, cups his shaggy breasts in his palms. He has bigger boobs than some women he knows. They have to jiggle when he runs. Along with his jowls and his belly and his butt, his cock wagging its own frantic dance as he lopes along. The thought makes him never want to move again. At least not quickly. Nothing more than a slow, muscle-bound walk, which he practices a few steps of and stops because it hurts his back.

Reconsiders

What else can you expect of a fifty-year-old? Flesh sags. Gravity can't be denied. You have to go with the flow, right? But it's not all bad. He is, by his own admission, in the best shape ever. He can run five miles with little, if any, discomfort other than a touchy ankle. He plays tennis, holding his own with men ten or fifteen years his junior. He feels at the height of his intellectual and creative powers. He is at least tolerated and maybe even respected at work. As far as he can tell, his wife still loves him, and other women don't run away in horror when he approaches. All of which reinforces his own view that what he sees in the mirror doesn't reflect the person he imagines himself to be from the inside looking out.

Works

So it's not what he thought he would be doing when he was

fresh out of college and still had the rest of his life in front of him. Then he was going to set the world on fire with his sheer brilliance, his energy, his raw but undisputed talent with the written word. The Pulitzer Prize was his for the asking. Maybe even the Nobel. His star would rise high and hold firm, and he would enter middle and old age as a sought-after sage, someone who could wax eloquent on the meaning of it all and be listened to.

But then he got hungry, got cold, became lonely, got married, had children, took responsibility for their lives seriously, got a job.

Like any other job. He goes, does it, comes home, eats, goes to bed, gets up, goes back, does it, comes home, eats—five days a week, forty-nine weeks a year. It's no worse than other things he's done. Not as bad as some, like cleaning chicken coops or pig pens or storage vaults in grain elevators, dangling by a rope in dust so thick you can't see the wall in front of you. Or roofing in a-hundred-and-twenty-degree heat. Or digging post holes along a fence line. Or cooking hamburgers in a fast-food joint. Or bagging groceries. Or counting money in a bank. Selling life insurance.

He's in purchasing. Making sure there are enough parts and containers and whatever else to keep the plant running smoothly. He and two other men he hardly talks to. He calls them Nut and Bolt, but not to their faces, and if he's not with them, he can't keep them straight in his mind, therefore the interchangeable names. All they ever discuss is money, food, whatever sport is current, and whether or not this or that woman is a nice piece of ass. But maybe he's boring, too. How could you not be when the majority of your day is taken up tallying fasteners and washers, toilet paper and towels, oil and grease, pens, paper, toner for the Xerox machine, plastic arms, legs, heads and eyes, mechanical voice boxes. They make toys. Cheap toys that you win at bazaars and carnivals. Probably dangerous toys that could injure or even kill young children, but that isn't his department.

Makes love

Slips into bed, his back to her, hand on the side of her hip, fingertips grazing flesh below the hemline of her nightgown, and although she doesn't move, he can tell by her breathing that she's still awake—something she does when she's waiting to see what his intentions are—so he slides his finger into the crease between hip and leg, and she gasps, rolling over and pulling him onto his back, knee sliding over his pelvis as he strokes her thigh, knee to hip, slowly over soft inside skin, and she umms, puts her arm around him, tongues his ear as he raises his hand to warmth and hair, her leg lifting for a better fit, and he slides on top, half straddling her so she can drive herself as tightly as she wants against his thigh while he pins her arms to the bed, kisses her mouth, neck, ears, her head twisting side to side, locked legs quivering, nightgown rising, nipples nut-hard between his teeth, legs releasing as she reaches for his penis, guides him into her, a perfect rhythm, like partners who have danced to the same song hundreds of times, point, counterpoint, swirl and glide, rising in tempo and tension until he thinks he might die, wouldn't care if he did, and then it's over, and he lies beside her saying, "I love you I love you I love you," meaning each word, for he has never felt so alive nor been so in love and wonders for a moment what difference there is between them.

Vanishes

Gone. Just like that, without a trace. Out of sight, out of mind, he'd like to say, but he can hear her from somewhere far off calling his name, wanting something, possibly even needing something, which makes him feel guilty, but not so much so that he would consider revealing his whereabouts. Feels like a kid playing hide-and-seek on a hot summer night, the screech of cicadas ebbing and flowing in rhythm with his own breathing, burnt grass and dry earth rising to mouth and eye as he lies face down in the streetlight shadow of a huge American elm tree, determined not to be discovered. Like Dagwood hiding from Blondie, in the closet, the attic, basement, garage, the neighbors', only to be led out by the ear sooner or later to do something that she has planned for him, him and her, all of them, a trip, a movie, shopping, dinner out, church, another day gone with nothing to show for it.

Runs

Same route each time. So he doesn't have to think how far he's gone, how far he has to go, and can concentrate instead on finding the right pace, his cruising speed, he likes to call it. Some days nothing's right—legs hurt, can't catch his breath, feet feel like bricks, air tastes like burlap—but today he could run forever, thumb his nose at the doubters who say with their eyes: Jim Fixx didn't think it could happen to him either. Right past death itself, a bird in the face, straight into that euphoric state he used to enter driving across the plains at night, Wolfman Jack howling all the way from Del Rio, Texas, no time or space, no distance to or from anywhere. Only music and the road as far as your headlights shone, the hum of the motor, warm summer wind in your hair, one foot after another, stride strong as a piston stroke, heart thumping a rich, steady beat, as the woman runner approaching you, body long and lean, ponytail bouncing, smiles when your eyes reach hers.

Goes to the doctor

So what if he wears reading glasses, his internist says, leaning back in his leather chair and peering at him across the desk from heavy-lidded eyes that make him seem perpetually sleepy or disinterested. So what if he can't hear as well as he used to. So what if a little arthritis is creeping in. He should feel thankful it's nothing more. His heart's fine. His lungs. His kidneys. Liver.

Colon. Prostate. You name it, it's—*he's*—fine. That doesn't mean they should be resting on their laurels, though. They need to keep on top of things, nip problems in the bud. Like his most recent blood workup, which showed HDL and LDL and triglyceride levels not at what they should be, and his blood pressure's up, his testosterone's down, New York, New York, it's a hell of a town. But nothing serious enough to require medication—*yet,* his doctor says. He can most likely still control it through weight loss. Stop eating, stop drinking, exercise more. His health is a serious matter, he's told. He's got a wife to think of. He's got kids. They need him. They want him around as long as possible. Prove it, he says, but the doctor isn't listening.

Takes a day off

Kills the alarm, goes back to bed. Listens to his wife shower and dress, wake the kids, feed them, come back to the bathroom— "You all right?" "Fine." "Aren't you going to work?" "No."— go down the stairs, gather books, backpacks, lunch money, leave to drive the kids to school, herself to the office.

And that's all? he's thinking in the still dim bedroom light. No "Haul your lazy ass out of bed and get moving"? No sit-beside-him, hand-on-his-forehead concern that he might be sick—or worse, suicidally depressed? Has he become so predictably unpredictable that nothing surprises her, angers her, saddens her, moves her to biting sarcasm? Could it be that she plain doesn't care anymore? About him? Them? That she has finally, as he's always feared, met someone else, someone so captivating that she has already abandoned him? Or is going to as soon as she gets to the office and can use her phone in private? Call him to say she's not coming back, then the other man to say it's over now, can they go for a drink? She cries, he holds her hands in his, they talk—what does he look like? tall, lean, wavy dark hair, good dresser, nice voice, a twinkle in his eye—she cries some more, he gives her his handkerchief, she smiles, they kiss, they go to his apartment. That's what he can't stand. Somebody else touching her, knowing her the way he does. Why? he wonders. Why not? Why hasn't it happened before now? What does he have to offer her no one else can? But what about the kids? What'll they do for a mother? And him? What'll he do—?

He folds his hands over his chest on top of the sheet, imagines himself in his coffin, looking out. At what? At whom? The boys,

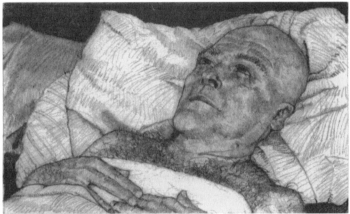

surely. They're there. And her, too, even if she is with someone else. The time they spent together can't have been all bad. They're talking quietly, hanging their heads, shedding a few tears, accepting condolences from old friends who took the time to stop by. So sorry, he hears. Such a pity. Such a loss. What on earth happened? Heart attack, they're told. Which satisfies them, but shouldn't, because it's not the truth. Here lies a man who died of frustration, he wants to tell them, but can't, of course. And even if he could, no one would want to understand how someone like him, with all that he has, could say such a thing.

Grow up, Bucko. Get up. *Carpe* fucking *diem*.

Cooks

Something nice, he's thinking. Just for them. The kids can

GARY D. WILSON

order Chinese, have hot dogs, grilled cheeses, whatever. Watch a movie. Stay out of their hair.

Something tried and true—no surprises—something they both like, but elegant, to go with candlelight, wine, flowers, slow music, quiet talk. And maybe more, as the ads say.

He decides on lemon chicken, rice pilaf, fresh green beans with toasted almonds, and, for dessert, kiwi slices on lime sherbet.

Which means shopping, of course, which he hates but will do if it has a purpose. Lumber, underwear, groceries on special occasions. He once bought a suit in four minutes. In and out, just like that. Quick, simple, satisfying.

Something he has no right to expect at Giant on a Saturday morning. But the drive over is surprisingly pleasant. No more than the usual number of crazies going too slow or too fast, tailgating, passing in right-turn-only lanes, one woman so old and bent her chin nearly rests on the steering wheel, paying no heed to anyone as she drives straight down the middle of the street, traffic backed up for a block behind her. And he finds a parking space in his favorite spot, only one person in line at the bank machine, a grocery cart without having to go back outside to retrieve one, and to top it off, the most beautiful woman he's seen in weeks, standing in the produce section as if waiting for him to arrive. Young, lithe, black hair braided to the middle of her back. Short-waisted red top, black tights, skin the color of the faintest pink rose, breasts swelling as she sighs at the green pepper in hand, shakes her head no, gold hoop earrings, a diamond stud in her right nostril. A tattoo? he wonders. Surely she has one. Something discreet in a discreet place—thigh, hip, breast—a flower or a butterfly that wings gracefully away when she drops the pepper in disgust and wheels her cart toward the dairy section.

He follows, maintaining his distance, doing his own hunting and gathering, but keeping her in sight, timing his forays so that

142   *Glimmer Train Stories*

he meets her head-on in one aisle, trails her down the next, each encounter allowing him to know her better. She's twenty-eight to thirty, probably had braces at one time, since no one is born with teeth that straight, isn't married or engaged—at least no ring or ring mark on her finger—may or may not have on underwear, but is wearing black shoeboots with a low heel and pointy toes, has a mole on her neck just under her left mastoid bone. In cereal, he discovers her name is Angela. Not because she's an angel. Far from it. Just like the aunt she's named after, who at forty abandoned her husband and children and ran off to Hawaii to become the person she always knew she was capable of being. In canned vegetables and pasta, he learns that this Angela, again like her namesake, has had lots of boyfriends, but none of them has treated her well, so she is generally suspicious of men and their motives—except for older men, of course, well-kept older men, whom she finds irresistible. In beverages, he discovers that she's Catholic and has never had a child, but has had an abortion, which she feels so guilty about she's sure she's going to hell. In pet food, he finds out she votes a straight Democratic ticket, supports most social welfare programs but also thinks welfare reform is a good idea. She works as an interior designer but paints Miróesque portraits in her spare time. At the deli counter, she reveals that she thinks she's too fat, her breasts are too small, hips too wide, eyebrows too heavy, skin too pale. She feels overworked, underappreciated, and stupid, and would welcome a kind word from anyone. He gives her one in paper goods and household supplies, telling her how lovely and deserving she is. She's so taken by his kindness that her eyes well with tears, and he pats her there there on the back and she asks how she can ever repay him and he tells her to think nothing of it and she says she can't do that, would he please come to her house for dinner, which he of course says of course to, and they eat and talk all along the meat section. By frozen foods, she has gone to freshen up and he finds her emerging from a hot shower, even more beautiful than he had imagined, and with his help, she towels off, wraps up, and disappears into her bedroom, presumably to wait for him.

They check out in parallel lanes, walk nearly together down the corridor of the little shopping mall, past the boutiques, the yogurt and book shops, the movie theater, straight to the liquor store, where he buys two bottles of burgundy—one for dinner, the other as a spare—and she gets a six-pack of Bud. There are two registers at the checkout counter. He is at one, she at the other. She looks at him, he at her, thinking how incredibly wonderful it is. "You know, we're going to have to stop meeting like this," he says. "What?" "The store? Now here?" he gestures vaguely. "Go fuck yourself, old man." With a flip of the head, she gathers up her bag and leaves, and they never speak to each other again.

Loses something

Same intersection as two weeks ago, same interminably red left-turn signal, same wiry man with tearful eyes, haggard face, trembling lips, scurrying from car to car, a small red plastic gas can in hand, as he tells what must be the same story about how his car's just run out of gas and his kids are home alone waiting for him and he can't call because there's no phone and they don't have a mother anymore and they must be worried sick by now, so anything, anything at all, will help. Two weeks ago, he believed him. The man told his story with such sincerity that all he could think of was those kids huddled together on a couch, wondering what had happened to their father, whether he'd been hurt in an accident or god knows what else, and he reached for his wallet and pulled out the only cash he had, a five-dollar bill, and thought how his grandmother would have approved because of the man's hands, honest hands, she would have called them, callused working hands you could trust, held out toward him—thank you, sir, god bless you, sir, you're so kind, you won't regret this—as he backed away, turned, and jogged off in the direction of the filling station.

He should be angry, he supposes, should call the police or something, should get out and yell to everyone not to listen to the man, he's a con artist and he'll only make a fool of them. Or maybe he should talk to the man, reason with him, explain how what he's doing isn't right and why. Or instead maybe he should applaud his creativity, since thirty years ago he was doing the same sort of thing, which they called guerilla theater, street theater, but for a cause, not money. Or maybe he should just laugh the whole thing off, grateful for any diversion that helps separate one day from another.

Or he could, which he does, sit right where he is, watching the man get closer and closer, and when he's about to lean down to make his pitch, say, "Sorry, but I already gave," and roll up the window, turn on the radio, and drive off, feeling not one bit satisfied and strangely sad.

Considers his future

—When, as a white male, he is one and a half times more likely to kill himself than to be killed by someone else.

—When men who are bald before age fifty-five have a significantly increased risk of heart attack.

—When forty percent of married men admit to having committed adultery, as do thirty-seven percent of married women.

—When, by retirement, he will have spent forty-three years at a job that has contributed no satisfaction or meaning to his life.

—When he has a greater chance of being struck by lightning than winning a lottery.

—When the tear in the ozone layer over Antarctica is increasing at such a rate that everyone on earth will soon look like a curly fry.

—When half of all marriages end in divorce, on average, seven years after the wedding.

—When men are, on average, stronger than women, but women become richer than men because they outlive them.

—When he is ninety-five times more likely to be killed in a car accident than a plane crash.

—When Harlequin romances, as a group, outsell every other type of book in America.

—When sex may never again be safe.

—When Texans possess thirteen point something firearms per person, regardless of age or gender.

—When it now takes working well into May before his total tax obligation is met.

—When he knows, but resents, that there is no such thing as a free lunch.

—When, because of pollution, thirty percent of American rivers and fifty percent of American lakes are not safe for swimming, fishing, or other uses. Such as drinking?

—When each of his children will cost about a quarter of a million dollars to raise.

—When, by the time his mortgage is paid up, he will have mowed his lawn seven hundred and twenty times, which will have consumed one thousand and eighty hours, or forty-five days, or one and a half months of his life.

—When twenty percent of the people around him in large groups are certifiably insane.

—When the two greatest human motivations remain greed and lust.

—When the sun will burn out in five billion years.

—When he has a hundred-percent chance, on average, of dying of something, somewhere, sometime.

Has a revelation

He lies in bed, trying to figure out what he did to prompt the need for four hundred dollars in overdraft protection at the bank. What kind of screw-up, what kind of shortsightedness, lack of focus, information, desire led to the error? And it's not the money that bothers him so much as the hassle. Because now he'll have to go to the bank. As soon as he finds the error. His, he assumes. Banks don't make errors. None that they've ever admitted to, at least. Not in his experience. So regardless of how honest his mistake was, he'll have to go to the branch and sit in their little reception area, hat in hand, waiting until one of the people at a desk deigns to see him, although they will have *seen* him for several minutes, and he'll have to tell them what happened and be made to feel like a complete idiot for doing something so stupid, all of which will be communicated by sidelong glances and twitching smiles, and in the end, as a final insult, he'll be required to pay interest on the money "loaned" to him. Not much—less than a dollar—a small amount compared to how much it would have cost him to have covered all the bounced checks. It's just the drabness of it, the business-as-usualness. It would be better—much more fun, exciting—to think someone had embezzled the money and was trying to conceal the act by saying he'd made a mistake. That would at least have some pizzazz to it. Except he can't imagine anybody going to the trouble of altering bank records for four hundred bucks, or even a thousand. Ten thousand, maybe. A hundred. Maybe then. But it would still depend on what the risks were. Jail, ostracism, loss of a hand, death by torment. Death? Die for money? No way. What for, then? What would he die for? His family? That's tough. He knows he's supposed to say yes automatically, without thinking, as a reflex. And he probably would, if push came to shove, in the passion of the moment, that sort of thing. When he wasn't thinking. So if not them, what: Who? Himself? How? It's still suicide, no matter how you look at it. Even if you die trying to save yourself, you're still dead. Although he has, he has to admit, thought about it. The peacefulness, the finality. Not ever being tired again or sick or in discomfort. Never having to get up and go to work. Never having to answer to anybody for anything. Never having to buy, repair, return another thing. Never having to cook or eat or wash or dress or brush your teeth, shave, shower, shit.

He hears his heart beating in his neck, behind his ear, and can't stand it and sits up, his face coming into dim view in the mirror opposite him, whump-thump/whump-thump/whump-thump, like factory noises in an old black-and-white film, a steam whistle about to go off. His head clears and he looks at himself and smiles at the recognition.

Celebrates

It's their anniversary. Their twenty-seventh. They haven't gone out because they're having people in the next night and need to get ready, so they're spending the evening cooking and talking. Which really isn't all that unusual. For them. They rarely do go out to celebrate. Except for their twentieth anniversary, when they went to London. Saw ten plays in seven days—Anthony Hopkins in *Lear,* Glenda Jackson in *The House of Bernarda Alba.* But as a rule they exchange cards, have a nice meal at home, maybe drink a bottle of champagne, nothing big. And that's the way it's been all along in their marriage. It just is, a fact of life, a way of life. They didn't even have a honeymoon.

He's chopping green peppers and onions at the counter on one side of the kitchen; she's stirring a sauce and waiting for water to boil at the stove on the other side. He's drinking a beer; she's sipping a glass of wine.

They've been chitchatting about flowers and the lawn, the kids, what they might do for vacation, when he tells her, for god knows whatever reason, in the midst of an otherwise pleasant and convivial evening, that their friends, Bill and Sylvia Harper, are splitting up after two kids and twenty-five years. That she either caught him or caught wind of him sleeping with another woman and asked him what the hell was going on and he said what and that it had been for quite a while and he didn't know whether he loved her or the other woman more, and she gave him the rest of the week to get his stuff out of the house so he could go somewhere else to think about it.

Stupid! his wife says, whacking the spoon handle on the rim of a pan. What a waste. What a jerk. What an idiot, moron, asshole, and he says she shouldn't be so harsh, since they really don't know the details and, given the right circumstances, the same thing could probably happen to anybody. And she laughs, but not humorously, and asks if he means like he caught a virus or something and couldn't help himself? Temporary insanity, temporary lust? He doesn't laugh, but he doesn't say anything, either, and she finally tells him it's all right, he might have a point after all, since there has to be something to account for how easily a man can be turned into a fool once he passes fifty. And he says thanks, and she says she isn't talking about him, and he says but he is fifty, and she says she'd better not be talking about him, and their eyes lock for a moment before he looks away and she says because she'd rather not believe he was that predictable, that he would get it on with some twenty-five-year-old who looks great but thinks shoe shopping is the height of intellectual activity. She deserves better than that, she says, and he nods absolutely.

But she either doesn't get the joke or doesn't want to acknowledge it, as she peers at him through her wine glass, sets it down and asks why they're even talking like that. It's silly, crazy, two people who've been together so long, done so much, loved so much. What sense does it make?

He raises his eyebrows and wiggles his head that he has no more idea than she has, and she opens the cupboard, takes out a box of pasta, pauses before putting it into the boiling water. He knows what's on her mind: If this can happen to them, to Bill and Sylvia, then who's safe? But he doesn't want to think about it or talk about it anymore and tells her he's ready to do something else to help before she has a chance to ask.

Sums up

A friend of theirs who is also a lawyer has been after them to make a will. To have some record of what they want done with their things, their money, themselves, for that matter. He won't even charge them, just fill out a couple of forms, get it done before it's too late.

But where to start? The money, what there is of it, is easy. Divide it straight down the middle. The house—sell it, split the profit. Or one buy out the other's half and live in it. They can decide that. Same with the furniture. The cars. Christ, how much stuff they have. Clothes, books, CDs, tapes, dishes, silverware, tools, paintings, photographs, a couple of computers, his old manuscripts—what about them? who'd want them? who'd care?—not to mention all the shit in the attic and basement. A lifetime of junk that doesn't mean a thing to anybody but them. The kids, maybe, in a couple of cases. The wooden cradle he built by hand before their older son was born. There might be some discussion over that. The electric-train set. But all the rest, they can do whatever the hell they want with it. Sell it for what they can, throw it out. Except his books. His special ones. The painting she did and one or two others they bought together, some letters he kept over the years. And, damnit, the manuscripts. Because there—as bad, as few, as insignificant as they are—is where anyone who wants to take the time will find him, who he was, what he thought, what he stood for, why he bothered. So those few things, maybe, although the truth is there's nothing of intrinsic value in even them, and they should probably be pitched along with the rest.

Concludes that

After he and his wife are gone, the love they've shared will be gone as well, because it's inside them, between them, and it doesn't travel. All that will then be left of his life that means anything can be found in the two pictures of him on his desk in the study. Not him alone; there are none of him alone anywhere. The first is of him and his older son, just after he brought mother and baby home from the hospital. He's holding his son, and his wife is beside him smiling at the baby with a look of relief and pride and trepidation only a new mother can muster, the three of them huddled together on the couch in a nice picture, a pretty picture, a perfect family sort of thing. His son was little and wrinkled then, eyes squeezed shut, left hand clenched in a tiny fist. His wife's hair was long, framing the profile of her face. He had a beard, full, dark brown, and soft, too, as he remembers. Not a hint of gray—in the beard or in his hair, which he had much more of at the time, although you can definitely see a bald head in the making. He was thirty-five; she was thirty-three. Children were her idea, he likes to say, even though when she asked what he thought, he didn't protest in any real way, didn't say no, not now, not ever. And he certainly didn't withhold his contribution to the process. Gave it eagerly, in fact, as enthusiastically as ever, and was shocked by the rapidity with which it produced results. First one son, then another, whom he's with in the second picture. He's in a car, their old yellow Rabbit, the door open, his son standing shirtless by it, both of them peering out at the camera. The title in the frame above the picture says in bold red letters: FATHER OF THE YEAR ACCLAIMED. The same father some of his son's school friends thought was his grandfather. An unfortunately honest mistake. His beard was what led them astray. In the ten years since the first picture, it had gone well past pepper to salt. Made him look sixty-five instead of forty-five. Time told in whiskers. In the faces of his children, where every day he can see more and more of himself emerging. As he fades, they grow. His years become their years, his life their life. At some point, they will be all of him that remains, and he hopes they're happy with it.

The Last Pages

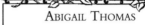

ABIGAIL THOMAS

*H*ere is a doodle I saved for reasons unknown. I think I was working at the time in an office that was actually a converted closet, into which they had managed to cram a desk and a wastebasket and me. I was a terrible secretary, but I got to watch the history-of-art class which met in the room I adjoined, and there I learned about perspective.

*L*ast year, I began to try to write a family history. But not a traditional history. The means of telling was as important to me as what I actually needed to tell. I needed a form in which the voice-dance of family knowing and not-knowing, telling and not-telling, was at least somewhat reflected on the page. So this happened: *My father writes; I write.* The truth, I think, lies somewhere in between our voices.

I didn't tell my father what I was doing for a long time. I was embarrassed about all the sex, and not quite sure how he would react to seeing his great great grandmother *shtup* the local baker. So I procrastinated until, finally, the book started to look like a book, and I realized that it wasn't right to hide it from him any longer. He was, thank goodness, very pleased. Actually, I think he was more amused that his adult daughter was embarrassed to talk to him about sex than the least bit disturbed about what I had done to his great great grandparents. He gave me a big hug. We enjoyed a good laugh.

Challah—traditional Jewish bread. My American grandparents are master bakers. My grandfather baked the bread in this photograph. And since "Esther and Yochanan" is a story about a baker …

My father on a botanical trip to the Dead Sea, circa 1957.

154

I was a late bloomer and it would be safe to say that I did not come into my own, did not revel in life for extended periods, until I was in my mid-twenties. When I was young, because I was so regularly insecure, I always felt myself the victim—every leaving was a personal affront, every end another sign of fundamental flaw. I have since then assumed I have some effect on the world, and realize that the comings and goings of the people around me are due as often to passion as indifference, self-protection as repulsion. And I speak as much of friends as of lovers—we can't underestimate the intensity and heartbreak friendships entail. Love is love. As to a third category of people who touch us— I've been lucky, my family has always been there. Ten, fifteen, nearly twenty years later I am looking back over incidents and see that I, too, caused pain, that I've been doing it all along. The thing about feeling you have a presence in the world, are as much inflictor as sufferer, is that you must relinquish your innocence, acknowledge that in the multitudes you contain, is an ignorant little germ.

*T*his is a photograph of my mother. My idea is that it was taken on a boat out on some ocean, in a blur of wind, a happy time. I include it here because I am fond of it, and because, for me, the likely unnoticed absence of a mother in this recent story—Celia's mother, and Kate's—is, at least in part, what compels the telling of it. In life, Mother's absence contributed to things happening as they did. In the story, events are distorted, recomposed, seen with an eye trained to shadow, to deficiency and revulsion; I acknowledge this. It's a bleak view, stingy even—selective, but not fabricated, not malicious. The house is the house where my sister lived. She will, no doubt, recognize herself, her husband, her child, her sister—who is a composite of both myself and our younger sister. She will remember that we dug up iris one sunny afternoon. And she will feel, I am afraid, misused, and as though others she loves were misused. I don't know what to say to this; I never do.

156

I remember the first time I ever saw snow. I'd only been in the States for a week, and one morning I woke up and found a whiteness over everything. I was utterly at a loss to explain it. Couldn't really capture *that* moment in this story, but I was able to provide a pretty accurate account of my first months in the United States. Since only my father could speak English, we depended on him a lot in those early months. I think he sort of enjoyed the power he held over us. I still grimace in autumn, when the leaves begin to lose their green.

Here I am with my agent. She made everything possible.

GARY D. WILSON

The "A Middle-Aged Man" story is an obvious distillation of lots of life experience, which all stories are. There is no single inspiration for the piece. It is, rather, a compilation of what, taken separately, might seem unrelated events, but which in my mind became interwoven and finally whole. You could even call it a meditation rather than a story in the usual sense of the word. An examination of a stage of life that was at once liberating and sobering, feelings which any honest look at existence is likely to produce. On a purely practical note, though, thoughts of writing a story about this character at mid-life were the result of an earlier piece I did, titled "To Himself on His Thirtieth Birthday." And since I'd recently turned fifty ...

PAST CONTRIBUTING AUTHORS AND ARTISTS
Issues 1 through 18 are available for eleven dollars each.

Robert H. Abel • Steve Adams • Susan Alenick • Rosemary Altea • A. Manette Ansay • Margaret Atwood • Brad Barkley • Kyle Ann Bates • Richard Bausch • Robert Bausch • Charles Baxter • Ann Beattie • Barbara Bechtold • Cathie Beck • Melanie Bishop • Corinne Demas Bliss • Valerie Block • Harold Brodkey • Danit Brown • Paul Brownfield • Evan Burton • Gerard Byrne • Jack Cady • Annie Callan • Kevin Canty • Peter Carey • Carolyn Chute • George Clark • Dennis Clemmens • Robert Cohen • Evan S. Connell • Tiziana di Marina • Stephen Dixon • Michael Dorris • Siobhan Dowd • Eugenie Doyle • Wayne Dyer • Mary Ellis • James English • Tony Eprile • Louise Erdrich • Zoë Evamy • Michael Frank • Pete Fromm • Daniel Gabriel • Ernest Gaines • Tess Gallagher • Louis Gallo • Kent Gardien • Ellen Gilchrist • Peter Gordon • Elizabeth Graver • Paul Griner • Elizabeth Logan Harris • Marina Harris • Daniel Hayes • David Haynes • Ursula Hegi • Andee Hochman • Jack Holland • Lucy Honig • Linda Hornbuckle • David Huddle • Stewart David Ikeda • Lawson Fusao Inada • Elizabeth Inness-Brown • Andrea Jeyaveeran • Charles Johnson • Wayne Johnson • Elizabeth Judd • Jiri Kajanë • Hester Kaplan • Wayne Karlin • Thomas E. Kennedy • Lily King • Maina wa Kinyatti • Marilyn Krysl • Frances Kuffel • Anatoly Kurchatkin • Victoria Lancelotta • Jon Leon • Doris Lessing • Janice Levy • Christine Liotta • Rosina Lippi-Green • David Long • Salvatore Diego Lopez • William Luvaas • Jeff MacNelly • R. Kevin Maler • Lee Martin • Eileen McGuire • Gregory McNamee • Frank Michel • Alyce Miller • Katherine Min • Mary McGarry Morris • Mary Morrissy • Bernard Mulligan • Abdelrahman Munif • Sigrid Nunez • Joyce Carol Oates • Tim O'Brien • Vana O'Brien • Mary O'Dell • Elizabeth Oness • Peter Parsons • Annie Proulx • Jonathan Raban • George Rabasa • Paul Rawlins • Nancy Reisman • Anne Rice • Roxana Robinson • Stan Rogal • Frank Ronan • Elizabeth Rosen • Janice Rosenberg • Jane Rosenzweig • Kiran Kaur Saini • Libby Schmais • Natalie Schoen • Amy Selwyn • Bob Shacochis • Evelyn Sharenov • Floyd Skloot • Lara Stapleton • Barbara Stevens • William Styron • Liz Szabla • Paul Theroux • Abigail Thomas • Randolph Thomas • Joyce Thompson • Patrick Tierney • Andrew Toos • Patricia Traxler • Christine Turner • Kathleen Tyau • Michael Upchurch • Daniel Wallace • Jamie Weisman • Ed Weyhing • Lex Williford • Gary Wilson • Terry Wolverton • Monica Wood • Christopher Woods • Celia Wren • Jane Zwinger

What a collection!

I rarely took showers, often forgot to brush my teeth, and wore the same dingy, rat-holed underwear for weeks. Besides all that, I was sneaky, willing to lie whenever, and a peeping Tom. I must have had some good qualities, but they don't occur to me at the moment.

from "Monsters" by Edward Falco

With all the freedom in the world—they say now there's more freedom in Russia—but if you don't have food at home for your family, freedom doesn't mean anything. The whole lifestyle is just not for humans. It's for dogs. Even my dogs, now, live better than we used to live in Russia.

from an interview with Aida Baker by Linda Davies

Washing dishes one night I hear Kathy's screen door slap shut and before I know it she's running up our back steps, calling "Skip, Skip!" then through the open door till she's standing in my kitchen. Intruder, alien. "Sorry," she says, going for the door that leads to the hall and Skip's place. "No time to go around."

from "Neighbors" by Melanie Bishop

I feel I reach into something quite directly. I was just saying to my editor the other day that it would be a while if ever again he got a book like that from me because I wasn't sure I could go to that area again. It's grim, straightforwardly grim. Unrelenting. I'm not sure I can do it again. Of course, I always say that and then I do it again, when I really felt like I couldn't do it again. When I'm writing, there is no distance between my writing and me.

from an interview with Jamaica Kincaid by Linda Davies